MY ROMEO

Leon Gratton

Grosvenor House
Publishing Limited

This book is published by
Grosvenor House Publishing Ltd
Link House
140 The Broadway, Tolworth, Surrey, KT6 7HT.
www.grosvenorhousepublishing.co.uk

A CIP record for this book
is available from the British Library

ISBN 978-1-80381-434-6

CHAPTER 1

Romeo was waiting in his clapped-out car. He was waiting for his lover, Julie to come out of the store. He wrung and cracked his manicured hands whilst staring at a couple of young girls who were buying magazines from the counter.

His sky-blue eyes lazily wander off the girls and onto his lover, with her dark brown hair and her uplifting walk. "She's laughing," he thought as she came to be served. He liked her laugh, it swam through the air most nights, he watched her come closer with the box of shopping.

"Treats for dinner gorgeous?" She smiled winked and put the box on the back seat. The weather was warm so he had the windows rolled down, he reached over and lifted up a pair of black Ray-Bans and put them on. Julie sat down and smiled through the sun. Her skin was natural, she wore no make-up and had a radiant smile which shone in her eyes all the time. They drove home with the radio playing.

*

Further out in the city an escape was in progress. Two men, John Carson and Sam Snide, two very evil and twisted men. They stood in the infirmary armed with butcher's knives and meat cleavers dripping with blood. Their faces were half grins and half grimaces, they had just hacked three guards up and had a fourth ready who was begging for his life.

"Kill him Sam," John said in a gravelly Snarl.

Sam didn't wait. He was tough, but John was totally fucking gone. So he walks right up to the Grovelling guard and as the man cowers, holding his hands out Sam swipes with his meant cleaver and takes two fingers off. Then with the butcher knife he stabs the man repeatedly. The two men start chopping and stabbing the shrieking guard. Chunks of flesh and blood cover the area like butchers' aprons. It becomes worse. Sam stops, but John carries on for a moment longer. Sam picks up the guard's keys, used to let the ambulances in and out.

"Come on John we got to get out of here before every fucker in the land is here."

There in the parking bay was the doctors car. "Come on Sam," John said as he turns the motor over.

*

Two days later the news is all over the papers. "TWO PRISONERS ESCAPE LEAVING CARNAGE" Romeo looks at this just as there is a knock on the door. Julie goes to answer the door as it is swung open and in walk the maniacal figures of John and Sam.

Sam grabs at Julie and says, "Where you going hon?"

She makes it past Sam but John grabs her before she can make it through the door. He grabs her and starts to the clothes off her. Romeo grips the seat he's on. Ready to pounce, half in fear half in anger. Sam walks right up to him and begins to wrestle the man into a piggy position.

"Pretty boy aint he honey?"

Julie squirms as the large man begins to sodomise Romeo. John carries on ripping the clothes off Julie. All that was going through Romeo's head was "Dead they're fucking dead". But the nightmare had just started. Sam, after finishing with Romeo turned Romeo's head and made him watch as John raped and beat Julie. Romeo looked on wondering whether they would let them live, but then it occurred to him they would be better off dead.

"Kill us you fuckers. Kill us so we don't have to see your faces."

"Oh you'll remember us for the rest of your life." Julie screamed when John said this as he pushed further into her. "Romeo we'll be okay. Romeo make him stop!"

Sam was inside Romeo again. This time with a butchers knife to his throat. "Yeaaah piggy wheee you seen *Deliverance* boy?"

Romeo's back passage was burning and bleeding. Sam was laughing. When John had finished with Julie he got up, whilst she just lay there the energy completely gone from her.

"You a good piggy boy?" The question didn't matter he spat on Sam who began to stroke the butchers knife under his eyes. "I should blind you Pig boy".

Romeo collects the mucus in his throat and spits on Sam. Sam grips his head in one of his gigantic hand and plunges it into his right eye.

The blood and puss spurt along Sam's arm. John laughs at the shrieking form of Romeo, who cups his hand over the wound as the blood began to spill onto the floor. They then dragged Julie through the kitchen and start to beat and douse her in petrol. Then as they walked out the door they lit a book of matches and threw them at Julie shouting as they left, "it aint over 'til the skinny lady burns".

Then there was hysterical laughter as they mounted their choppers and split. Then Romeo rolled over hearing the sirens come closer.

*

Two years later and Romeo is visiting the grave of his beloved. Tears streaming from his eye, a single red rose in his hand. He kisses the rose in his hand and puts it on the angel figure.

"Julie my angel I miss you," He whispers these words into the wind and sobs.

"They still haven't caught Sam and John."

Two things emerged after the atrocity. One, Julie was a month pregnant, and two, Sam had HIV and now so did Romeo, "it won't be long honey." The wind blows his long blonde off of his eye patch. "I'll be with you soon but not until I seek my revenge, especially for you and especially for Terry."

He had named their unborn child. The councillors and doctors had all advised against the naming of the child. But he was a ticking time bomb, he started visiting Dojo's and tattoo parlours. Fuelling his desire for revenge. He quickly became adept in Jujitsu. Karate and Ninjutsu. He knew his anger would consume him but he had vowed to his dead wife and unborn son that Sam Snide and John Carson would die He collapsed into a fit of despair by his wife's headstone.

Dragons lair in the city was where he headed next. He was going to forget, to let his body tell the symbolic story of his life, of how he had been enslaved by the two headed dragon which was chasing the very essence of him, his soul. He lay there on the bench while Denny, his tattoo artist, scribed more scales onto it.

"How you today Romeo?"

Romeo came out of his trance and let the wave of endorphins go, "You know what day it is Denny?"

Denny smiled and said, "Yeah it's Tuesday man, The third day of the month, the day you always come out here why?"

Romeo's dragon was bleeding on its tail. Where Denny was working. Denny stopped smiling and lay the tattoo gun down.

"Two years today," Romeo said.

Denny knew the man really well, especially the hurt in the man when he first met him. "Sorry man forgot."

Romeo closed his eye to stifle a tear. "They still out their man?"

Denny loaded a fresh needle on the gun. "They're still out their man,"

Denny swabbed away another patch of blood. "Good I'd hate for them to be caught."

Later that night Romeo headed for his ninjutsu class. With his Shuriken, Katana and Hanbo, a short staff slightly longer than an Escrima stick.

His tattoo's where hurting, but this never stopped him from going to his martial arts. He arrived and his sensei was warming up. Romeo bowed before entering the dojo. He lay down his kit bag and went and spoke to the sensei.

"Stephen?" the sensei stopped his warm up and walked over to Romeo.

"How are you Romeo?" he asked.

Romeo looked around the dojo and noticed the class had swollen. "Fine Stephen, new recruits?"

Stephen laughed, "Yeah and let's hope a few of them last huh?"

Romeo smiled, "Listen Stephen I need to get focused, can you give me a Nenriki lesson?"

Stephen smiled and gestured for Romeo to follow him. He led Romeo to an upstairs room where he took most advanced students. For special meditation. Then he led Romeo to the room out at the rear of the building. In it were two large oriental rugs with mystical symbols and pictures to focus on.

Also, in the room there was a shrine to Buddha that Stephen gave offering and thanks to.

"You remember the Ketsu- in?" Romeo nodded and sat in half lotus position. They began.

CHAPTER 2

Two days later, it's night-time and the rain is bucketing down. A bar southside of the city, two men walk in and grab a young girl. They match the descriptions of John and Sam. Romeo hears the alert over his scanner. He's out there within the hour, black and covered, hood, gauntlets and the sword strapped to his back. He's wired, psyched and ready. He starts by checking the alleyways around. Seeing if anyone's creeping around. He spots a van three block's shaking and moving, loud music, he thinks he can hear screaming. He slides along the wall keeping in the vans blind side.

Yep definite screaming. He draws closer and looks through the back window. Two heavily built men raping a young girl. Romeo snarls draws his Katana and opens the door, grabs the man on top and slides his sword across the man's throat. The blood splashes all over the girl and the other man. Who is sat with a can of beer. Then Romeo's hand, the hand that had held the man's head, flashes forward and the man gurgles on his own blood with a look of pure shock.

"Thank you," The girl say's gaining composure.

Romeo smiled under his hood then vanished.

Two nights later. Romeo has slipped into a dream state. His dreams are haunted by blood. He twitches and his dragon appears to growl. "You seen *Deliverance* boy? Wheee wheee. Ride that piggy."

Sam snarls in his face then turns into the red dragon. Then John appears with Julie strapped onto his back. Then he turns into the black head of the dragon. And starts to burn Julie with his breath. Romeo wakes up screaming, sweat lashing down his back. He gets up and goes to the closet and puts on a silk Kimono.

Then he breaks down and sobs. "Julie, I miss you." He whispers to himself, "I want you back so much."

He lays back down and remembers the good days with her, when suddenly he hears a voice distant yet friendly. "Romeo My Romeo I love you. I know you are in a dark place now my love, but we'll be together soon."

Romeo stirs again in his slumber, "Julie, Julie You are here."

The voice stills for a heartbeat then sounds again, "Yes Romeo I'm here."

"Take me with you Julie. I want to leave and be with you."

Julie's voice saddens, "You've entered a realm Romeo. The dragon's not your only demon."

Then suddenly his scanner blurts out a name which goes through Romeos heart like a dagger. "Possible Homicides in the Malibu estate, Culprit Sam Snide." Romeo sat bolt upright.

*

One hour earlier a chopper pulled up outside the Malibu estate owned by one Carlton Malibu. A wealthy lawyer with known mob ties. The man gets off the chopper and produced a machete and a 9mm Beretta.

"Wheee pigs I'll huff and I'll puff Wheee. Time for you to pass on Carlton."

He then walks up to the door and presses the bell. And after a short while it's answered by a butler. Sam points the pistol. And blasts the old, coloured man, who lands a few feet into the hall. He then walks over the new corpse and goes into what must be the lounge. He looks at a young fourteen-year-old. He brushes his dirty blonde hair out of his eyes then charges up to the boy and hacks him to bits. As he cuts into the teenager he screams, "Wheee piggy I'm going eat you all up."

The boy squealed as the weapon bit into him, blood covering Sam's denim jacket. He screams and squeals for a few seconds. Then at the doorway stands Carlton Malibu with a small snub nose Remington revolver.

"You're dead fucker!" He says but Sam is quicker, he whips up the 9mm and shoots Carlton in the face turning it into mush. Bursting the large capillaries and sending the pink tissue of his brain all over the wall behind him.

Sam walks out the living room and heads up the stairs. "Whee I wonder if there are any sows up here?"

He licks his lips as he climbs the stairs. He gets to the top when the alabaster ornament on the top stair railing blasts to bits. He turns in the direction it came from and see's Margarete, wife of Carlton Malibu brandishing a pump action shotgun. He looks at her maliciously. Then runs at her, she drops the gun then tries to lock herself in a room. Sam kicks in the door and grabs her, as he does so he hears a small voice "Mommy!"

Sam looks into her eyes, smiles and says. "Ahh a piglet whee haa."

There are loud screams that echo not only in the house but in the general neighbourhood.

*

Romeo sneaks round the area and sets his disguise. He's dressed in a dirty overcoat which he purchased from a homeless gentleman with a large meal and a similar coat. His fake beard looks grotty and his hands have been dipped in dirt. He crosses the police barrier coughing and staggering. A Young policeman walks up to him, "Sir You're going to have to leave, this is a crime scene."

Romeo carries on towards the house. The policeman puts himself in front of Romeo blocking his path. Just as the officer did so a detective spotted Romeo and excused himself from the conversation he is having. He walks across to Romeo and the young officer, "It's okay Mikey, I'll deal with the gentleman".

The young policeman leaves whilst shaking his head.

"Sir do you come from around here?" The detective says to Romeo. Romeo coughs and in a gravelly voice says, "No sir I just arrived yesterday. Came off cow freight."

"I'm detective Rolson. Can I ask you a few questions?"

Romeo shrugged "Sure".

The detective took out a note book.

"Though last night I was pretty gone sir," Romeo continued.

"I know I can smell it," He then motioned for the man to move to a quieter area. He stopped a young cop on his way to an unmarked car. "Could you get some coffee and some doughnuts?" He then looked at Romeo and said, "What happened to the eye and what's your name?"

Romeo touched the eye patch and said, "machine accident and my name is Ronnie."

They sat down in the car. Romeo waited until the man relaxed, then with quick reflexes he inserted a small electronic ear into the seat.

"Right sir where were you between 8.30pm and half past nine?"

Romeo looked at the man and started to think. 'Wasn't it 11.30pm when the call came through somethings wrong' He scratched his false beard, hiding his thoughts, "well sir I was sleeping around the Arches. With some cheap vodka for a pillow." He coughed.

The Detective, Rolson handed him a coffee and opened a box of doughnuts. Which had been handed to him when he got to the car.

The cop questioned Romeo for an hour, then gave up, giving him the doughnuts and a card with his office number.

Romeo headed away in search of somewhere to sleep rough.

Later that night, Romeo slips an earpiece in and listens to the conversation that's going on in the car. Between the detective and who looks like his superior. "Well Carl this is definitely a hit."

Carl Rolson, The detective sips his coffee.

"Shit Carl I thought Sam Snide was crazy but that shit with the four-year-old is sick."

Carl nods and says something like "fucker" then carries on sipping his coffee before he decides to speak, "Look boss, him and John are working for some mean fucker southside who has killed four pushers."

The other man snorts and sits still.

"Come on, I mean what do you think happened to the Latino brothers who cook for Gonzales's?"

The other man carries on nodding, and sipping his coffee. "Then Gonzales turns up all carved up. And they are all on Malibu's pay roll."

The other man replies, "John and Sam may be going big for themselves."

Detective Rolson suddenly bangs the dashboard. "Shit boss he gutted that four-year-old. He continues to pound the dashboard.

"What did forensics Say Carl?"

Carl looked at the boss. "Same shit Boss Sam Snides prints everywhere and no weapon. Though' they did find a small trace of his blood. It was at the top of the stairs It had large traces of LSD in it."

They went quiet as if there was something vital there. Romeo took out the earpiece and sits on his haunches and smiles and thinks 'Sam is on mind altering drugs. He'll fuck up somewhere.'

Two days later Romeo is stumbling past the Malibu residence. Carrying bags, and watching two cops who are sitting outside in a police car. He decides to take a look inside. He stumbles around the back of the house, unnoticed. He slips out of the large jacket and hole-covered jumper. Underneath he is wearing his full ninja Gi. He slips his hand into one of the bags. And produces the hood and the black sash to cover his mouth. He puts them on then stashes the jacket and bags under a bush. Then, like a cat he searches for the shadows. And creeps into them and slides along the wall avoiding the daylight. He finds the servant's back entrance which is locked. He pulls out a small pouch with which has several long serrated and pointed instruments he slips two of them into the lock and quickly has it open.

Romeo enters the house and starts to scout around, looking at the chalk drawings of the victims. He then looked at the placement of bullets. Then he decides to find out how connected Carlton Malibu was.

He walks upstairs and enters what looks like the study. He goes straight to the desk that has been upended, leaving all the documents and papers scattered around the room. He started to sift through the documents looking for key names or anything that might ring a bell. He came across two documents about two companies in the construction business that are being sued. Although the party that was suing them was unnamed, these companies are both owned by the Grimaldi family.

'Costa Nostra' Romeo whispers to himself.

Just then the front door opens and Romeo stumbles slightly. The cop hears Romeo and draws his revolver then starts up the stairs. Romeo conceals himself at the side of the doorway. The policeman who is inexperienced points his revolver into the room and says, "come out with your hands up."

Romeo produces a packet of Metsubushi (blinding powder) and blows it into the policeman's eyes. Then quickly moved down the stairs. And back out, locking the servant's door behind him.

Later that day Detective Rolson is questioning the police Officer. "So, Mikey You called out the warning. Then you were blinded by this powder?"

The officer shuffled his feet, "Yes sir".

The detective looked at the report on his desk, then at the pictures of the two men who had grabbed the eighteen-year-old out a bar. "You never saw anyone or anything?"

Mikey shook his head, "No sir, just a feeling of blackness. I didn't even hear breathing".

Carl looks at the young man "Right you can go Mikey," The young officer turns to leave, "Mikey?" He stopped, "Check the sides of the door next time and radio for back-up."

Mikey leaves the office. And Carl carries on reading, "commonly used in Ninjutsu." Carl whispers the word "Ninjutsu" Then looks at the case of the two rapists in the van.

CHAPTER 3

Romeo decides to head away from the Malibu residence. As now he was sure that this was bigger than random killing spree's. No, John Carson and Sam snide were working for someone, and Romeo had to find out who.

Later that night, whilst at home. Romeo is packing his kit away, and checking his weapons. His neck hair hackles up. And Romeo's Ki goes haywire. There is a flash outside his window and two men in black hoods crash through. He had been feeling, this was coming for a while, a rival ninja clan. Deciding to test out the Togakures top student. Romeo rose drawing his katana looking for signs of a move by the two dark figures in front of him. He saw a flash and a spinning shuriken flew at him. He reacted quickly and shifted his body weight and struck with his katana knocking the shuriken to the floor.

Then one of the ninjas produced a long chain. And sent it wrapping around Romeos wrist. Romeo changed sword hands and leapt as the ninja pulled on the chain. Meanwhile the other ninja had produced a Wakizashi and was slicing down whilst Romeo was parrying the one with the chain. Who was trying to pull Romeo off balance? Romeo shifted the odds by grabbing the chain and wrapping it around his katana and the other ninjas wakizashi, This sent the two-ninja crazy, whilst they were confused by the action Romeo slid his hand down to the hilt of his Katana and drew a throwing knife. Which he launched at the ninja with the chain. It went through the ninjas head killing him instantly. He now only had the ninja with the short samurai sword to deal with. He had dropped the sword and was now brandishing a tanto samurai dagger. He ran in with a slicing uppercut trying to push Romeo of guard. Romeo took the knife out the ninjas hand. The ninja recoiled and pulled out several shuriken, threw them at Romeo who dodged them all but one that caught him in the shoulder. The ninja then pulled out an impact flash bomb and threw it on the floor, distracting Romeo long enough to get out the window.

Romeo removed the shuriken, wincing and walked over to the body of the first ninja. He searched the man and found the usual arsenal and caltrops. But it was his climbing gear that interested. Romeo. They were claws used to grip stone and other hard surfaces. "Koga Ninja," he whispered to himself as he took out other things, poisons, Metsubushi powder and flash bombs.

Romeo picked up his phone and dialled Stephen his Sensai. It rang a while then Stephen's voice came over. "Hello?"

Romeo thought he sounded tired, then he looked at the clock and saw that it was three am. "Hi Stephen, Romeo here."

Stephen started to complain but soon listened as Romeo told him what happened. Stephen finally hung-up telling Romeo he'd be right over with help.

Romeo picked up the shuriken's and other weapons. And as he picked up the throwing stars he noticed that there was a sticky substance on them.

"Shit. Poison."

The poison was a lethal twenty-four-hour toxin according to Stephen, "Yeah there's a cure Romeo, but the Koga guard it well."

Romeo looked cross at himself for being sloppy. And started mulling over the opportunities.

Stephen carried on, "You could go on a long-term anti toxin that we develop. Or you can go across to Japan and get the immediate anti toxin which will leave a malaria like fever for a few days".

"Romeo looked at Stephen firmly and said, "Stephen you know my situation, you know I got to do both. You know I'm a walking time bomb. The Chinese herbs and acupuncture are only doing so much."

Stephen looked around, "Any leads on you know who?"

Romeo sighed, "Yes Stephen".

"They made another hit usual carnage no clues".

Stephen replied, "So that was Sam Snide in the Malibu hit".

Romeo stared into Stephens eyes. "How do you know it was Sam?"

Stephen smiled, "I've got contacts too. I also had a cop asking questions about two dead rapists". Romeo looked panicked, unnerved by the statement.

"Don't worry Romeo I told them nothing."

"You know us, we're very discreet." He put his arm around Romeo and gave a friendly squeeze. "show me the ninja's kit?"

Romeo opened the lock, whilst two of Stephen's students took the dead body out in plastic. Romeo took out the ninjas weapons and potions and handed them to Stephen. Stephen looked at them as they were wrapped in cloth.

"These are going in my collection."

Romeo was looking at the wound on his shoulder.

Stephen smiled and said, "I should get the herbs out and make a poultice for the wound, draw as much of the venom out as possible. Stephen smiled again and carried on. "I'll get the long-term anti toxin to you in the morning."

He turned looked out the window. He watched his people work the shadows with expert eyes. Then the signals to two young men walking out a local bar, one yawns then puts his fingers in his mouth and whistles twice.

"All clear but I think I will set up a few people to keep an eye on you ok?"

Romeo looks at the mess and say's "Take my kit to the dojo Stephen I want this place clean in case the cops show up."

Stephen nods whilst Romeo walks over and puts his suit and weapons in a black bag. "Romeo you should maybe go to Japan?"

Romeo looks at him, "You know you've worked hard and you know a lot about our Ninjutsu system. You could go over smooth things over between the Koga and Togakure?"

Romeo looks at Stephen and says, "Stephen I can't, Sam, and John..."

Stephen cuts Romeo short, "Listen Romeo you've got a Koga toxin in your blood. Someone is sending dark dreams through your door. And you are dying of Aids! Go there speak to the Koga, learn from them. They may even tell you who's contracting their guys. I mean for Christ sake it could be those psychos."

Romeo stands there nodding quietly weighing the pros and cons. Stephen walks up to the front door of the apartment and say's just as he was leaving, "Think about it Romeo Think about it".

Romeo looks on as Stephen leaves.

CHAPTER 4

The next morning Romeo is at breakfast waiting for the Anti toxin. He starts to look at things from the other view, the view that he's dying. And that he is killing people. He is in effect being Judge, Jury and Executioner. All for the sake of revenge. All for his bloody thirst to pay back those people who rape, kill and oppress the weak. There's a knock on the door. He collects the herbal tablets form the young oriental. Then sits back down to his breakfast.

Later in the afternoon he heads to his tattoo studio to get some work done on his dragon, his pain, envy and tragedy. The pain he doesn't mind as it is washed away in endorphins. While he envies the death of his lover as it saved her from the agony. The tragedy, well the tragedy has happened and has scarred his very soul so the dragons scales, it's essence, the heads of each one circling his soul turning his inner pain into living art. He lays there on the table listening to the buzzing of the needle. He slips in and out of consciousness, the pain numbing his thoughts. Taming the savagery in his spirit.

Denny speaks, "Sam do that thing on the Malibu estate?"

Romeo wakes slightly, "Yep!"

Denny mutters a curse word and carries on colouring the flames surrounding the black dragons head, "Have you heard anything Denny?"

Denny smiles, "No man".

Romeo slips back into his trance.

"But I hear there is a new gang in town. They've been buying everything and taking out the old bosses".

Romeo lifted his and nodded, "yes, Denny I know this. But what I don't know is who they are."

Denny dipped the nib in the paint and carried on with the colouring, "They're bikers, old school angels and such. They are acquiring every cutthroat around". The man looked round to make sure no one was in the shop. "The triangle."

Romeo lifted himself up slightly, "Who?"

Denny looked puzzle, "The triangle started by three guys that no one has seen".

Denny spat as he finished. Romeo lapsed back to a conversation he had heard whilst scouring around next to the Malibu residence. Two drunks had been talking the first one had said, "Some ones hiring for money".

The second one gave a small cough, "yeah I heard the triangle, they are trying out new cocktails for money. High and paid for it as well".

Romeo remembered this and started to think that this triangle was started by Sam and John. But even so who is the third person. Who's the string puller. Romeo lay back down concentrated on the buzzing again. Thinking back to the days when Julie and he were together. Slipping ecstasy instead of pain. The dragons needed a lot of work but he always took it to Julie. She was his fire and also the fire that burned in the belly of the two headed dragon.

He headed straight to the dojo after his tattoo session was over. He entered the building feeling the presence of one maybe two ninjas following him. Stephen summoned one of the other sensei to take over the class. He walked up Romeo, "You thought about Japan Romeo?"

Romeo looked over the class and saw they were training shuriken and small knives. He remembered his lessons in shuriken and small knives and smiled, "Yeah Stephen I've thought about Japan and I know it's risky but I'll go. I'll need watching over, there's lots of trouble in that climate".

Stephen nodded in agreement. "Yeah And the Koga are cautious, if they think you are trading there secrets they will kill any way they can".

Romeo had his eye on a young green belt, who was using his shuriken as a hand-held weapon. Romeo looked at the rest of the class who are wielding and throwing their weapons. "good class tonight Stephen".

Stephen smiled, "Yes Romeo your favourite part, Shuken throwing weapons".

Romeo again looked over the students and noticed one of the younger ones, "he's lacking power from the wrist. But his technique is solid enough though".

Stephen nodded and said, "Right Romeo I'll arrange everything for you to go across to Japan and meet with the Koga".

Stephen and Romeo headed up the stair's for a Nenriki session. They knelt this time, focusing the breath thought and hand movements.

Two days of meditation, after which Stephen arranged everything for Romeo to go to Japan. He finished the last Kirri in and Romeos breath left sharp like water flowing through a pipe. Stephen came through with a cup of Chinese tea.

"Everything is ready Romeo your plane takes off tonight. There will be people to meet you off the plane."

Romeo relaxed his hands and rested his concentration, "so is there equipment and stuff over there?"

Stephen went over to the buddha shrine and lit a stick of incense. He bowed to the shrine, then knelt next to Romeo.

"Romeo," he paused. "They arrested Sam And John,"

Romeo looked at the shrine "Where were they Stephen?"

Stephen sighed, "listen Romeo, they're caught. They'll be sent to the chair, it's over".

Romeo looked weary.

"They were in some sort of bikers dive, with a ton of weapons and a load of drugs," Stephen paused trying to think of the name of the gang. Then it came to him, "The triangle".

Romeo clasped his hands in front of him. "That's it two years of bloody revenge over and I didn't even get to look them in the eyes as they die."

Stephen looked sorry for Romeo feeling his pain, "Listen Romeo the Koga, they know this is dangerous but they took it from the Togakure a long time ago, we'd like it back".

Romeo closed his eye "And?"

Stephen carried on, "It has a certain herbal formula and several hidden secrets, ask them for the dragon scroll of Iga?"

Romeo sighed, "And if they don't want to give it back?"

Stephen shrugged, "Steal it".

Romeo nodded and stood up.

CHAPTER 5

Later that night at the airport as Romeo is heading to the departure suite, he can feel spies all over watching his moves, scrutinising his every action.

"Nagoya airport sir smoking or non-smoking?" Romeo looked shiftily around looking for signals "Smoking or non-smoking sir?" The receptionists asked again.

"Non-smoking please."

She handed him his tickets, "That'll be boarding lounge eight, have a nice flight sir".

He walked away whispering, "I hope so".

The flight was a long one, he arrived at Nagoya International Airport, and realised quickly that he was still being watched, this time he saw the subtle signalling between two spies as he left to go to his hotel, he got into a taxi and told the taxi driver to take him to his hotel, all the while he could feel the eyes.

"Part of the ninja body," he thought. "If they want me it'll be on my terms".

He got to the hotel and was greeted by ensigns of the Koga family, "Hello Mr Greene," the first one said.

He was a tall, broad Japanese man in a smart business suit. The other man was short with a friendly smile. Romeo was immediately receptive to both men.

"Call me Romeo."

The man in the suit took Romeo's hand, shook it and said, "Hello Romeo we are your guides and I hope friends in the beautiful city of Nagoya."

Romeo smiled, "When do I meet with the Koga Shidoshi?"

The small man seemed to smile all the more. Romeo took the small man's hand and shook it.

"I am Hatayami," He said, "And the rude man in the suit is Kiarri".

The small man was dressed in traditional clothes of feudal Japan and his eyes twinkled with a subtle sense of pleasure. Romeo spoke with the men for half an hour then headed to his room to sleep off his jet lag. Time was a strange thing he thought, especially when it came to travelling.

Sleeping, the nightmares returned, this time Sam and John were dressed as Japanese Theatre demons. They were eating Julie on a table. They were surrounded by tiger striped Ninja who were laughing.

Then her voice came through the dream, "Romeo you must save yourself".

Romeo started to reach out for her. Then suddenly he felt this pain in his eye. He woke and the pain was still there. He touched the cauterized wound of his eye and looked at his finger "Blood" he whispered, then he got up and went to his sink. And washed the wound. "I must have scratched my eye in my sleep," he thought to himself. He looked and sure enough he had scratched right down his eye. He put his patch back over the wound and lay back down again. This time he dreamed of nothing. He woke in the morning to his hotel room phone ringing, he answered it and on the other end was Kiarri.

"Hello Mr Greene, We are to take you to the Shidoshi today".

Romeo smiled, "Okay I'll be down in twenty minutes".

Kiarri hung up and Romeo went and got dressed. He slipped into a pair of cotton slacks and a white short sleeved shirt. He slipped a Kobutan key stick into his pocket, in case anything happened at the dojo's. He went down the stairs of the Nagoya International and saw Kiarri who was stood there with another man talking. "Somethings wrong here," he thought "The picture doesn't seem to fit".

Kiarri then signed some documents as Romeo got closer. Kiarri walked up to meet him, "Ready Mr Greene?"

Romeo nodded and they headed out to the limousine which was waiting outside.

*

They arrived at the Koga tiger dojo and headed up the stairs. Romeo was edgy as shadows flipped through doorways. He could hear Kia's echoing through the hallways. He was sure this was the biggest and loudest ninjutsu school he had ever been in.

"This is the Koga dojo's. We teach Karate, Akido, Jujitsu and others. Most students don't know they are training in the black arts".

Romeo listened intently. "Then they are selected discreetly and put through the Koga Tiger examinations".

Romeo looked at Kiarri and said, "What are the Koga Tiger Examinations?"

Kiarri smiled, "That is secret knowledge that is past down from Shidoshi to master to student".

Romeo decided the time was right, "Kiarri you know why I'm here".

Kiarri looked at the one-eyed ninja. "Yes Mr Greene, you are here for the cure of the Koga shuriken poison."

Romeo nodded then said, "I am also here to ask for one of our sacred scrolls back".

"Ahhh," said Kiarri. "The Togakure dragon scroll."

"Yes, That's the one," said Romeo hoping he would make it out of the Dojo's with his life, and the scroll. Then he could go back home, and hunt the hunters.

But someone had other plans outside the dojo. A small spying mission which had begun in America was about to move more into action. The three men slipped into an alley across from the Koga dojos and started to get there kit out of the trash can in which it had been hidden. They donned there black Gi's which had a large green snake running down the right arm of the Gi's. they moved in the shadows arming themselves, their mission to stop Romeo at all costs.

Romeo was introduced to an old man of about eighty, who was watching a training session, of young kids all practising Kenjitsu.

"Hello Mr Greene."

Romeo shook the old man's hand and bowed slightly. The old man gestured for Romeo to sit. Romeo sat down next to the old man and watched as two teenagers battled with bokken. The tallest of the two was gaining the advantage by shuffling forward with a series of blows. But the smallest of the two had a few moves to show. He shuffled back two strikes feinted one way then struck, his bokken hitting across the other student's mid-section as he did so he gave off a Kia. The sensei called the class to a halt and Romeo spoke to the old man. "you are The Koga Shidoshi?"

The old man merely nodded and sat there looking at the children. The class bowed and the small teenager who had been in the sparring, came over and bowed to the old man then hugged him. He then spoke, "You now have Taijutsu Shuzi".

The young boy bowed one more time then headed out the room.

"My great grandson Shuzi in Koga. He is lightning fast with Katana."

Romeo smiled, looked in the old man's soft almond shaped eyes. He saw peace and wisdom of almost a century of craftmanship. "I have come for two things Shidoshi.

The old man sighed, "sushi Mr Greene?"

The old man picked up a walking stick, "Do you like sushi Mr Greene?"

Romeo stood up next to the tiny frail man who looked as if he would break if you blew on him.

"Do not be fooled by my age Mr Greene. This body may be frail but it still has power,"

Romeo did not doubt it.

The old man continued, "My Granddaughter has prepared a meal of raw fish for us to eat".

Romeo nodded and they went upstairs.

*

The three ninja had begun their entrance to the Koga Dojo. They stealthily crept up the stairs listening at each door for an American Accent They got to near the top of the building when two ninja dropped out of nowhere. The first wrapped a garrotte around one of the Snake ninja. The other came slicing down doing three quick cuts. One across the ninjas-midsection one upwards to his neck and the third across his neck. The third ninja produced an automatic pistol and shot the ninja with the Katana. Suddenly from behind him came a red hooded Ninja who struck silently at the ninja with the pistol grabbing his chin and sliding a razor-sharp knife across the man's jugular, blood gushed out and landed on the floor. Romeo was standing when the shots went off and headed for the door when the old man had gripped his arm and held him back.

"Let our people deal with it," He said then sat down. "You must be very valuable to them for them to attack here".

Romeo looked bemused, "We have been tracking them since America".

Romeo got the idea, "So it was your spies that I saw signalling at Nagoya Airport".

The old man continued to eat his sushi. "I'm surprised you didn't figure it out sooner."

Romeo sat down just as the red hooded ninja entered. He bowed to the old man and looked cautiously at Romeo.

"We have dealt with the three men Shidoshi."

The old man nodded, "Who are they?" The old man asked the red hooded ninja.

"Osaki member's Shidoshi," the red hooded ninja opened his hand and an emblem with a seven-pointed shuriken. He then handed the emblem to the old .

"Hmmm descendants of the Lin Qua."

Romeo looked puzzled at this. So he asked, "Who are the Lin qua?"

The old man took a sip of his Saki and started to think deeply, "We must get you to our monastery".

Romeo knew that this was serious as they keep this place and its location a grave secret.

"Kiarri?" the old Shidoshi said as the man entered the room. "You must prepare Mr Greene, for the journey to our island."

Kiarri bowed and then Romeo and he left.

*

Two days later in the monastery Romeo lay on his futon wondering what to do next. Who were these Lin Qua and why were they so interested in him. The wooden and paper door slid open. And in walked three beautiful Geisha.

The first bowed and knelt next to him, "we are here to purify you for the Koga tiger tests." She then began to undress him. He protested at first, but soon realised they were only there to sponge him.

"What's the smell?" he asked politely as the vapour from the sponges which was acrid and sour smelling hit his nostrils.

"That is a mild numbing agent that we grow locally, it is to help with the first part of the test."

Romeo began to grow suspicious, "trust us, you are on holy ground".

They sponged him down then they brought in a large casket and started to wrap him in black and orange, around his wrists and ankles. Then they produced a ninja Gi of the same colours.

"You are Togakure so we will not insult you with our choice of weapons choose?"

She then pointed to the wall on the far end of the room. On which was every weapon a ninja could use. And even some Romeo had never seen.

"What is the test?"

"There is a man. An opium merchant who has disgraced us truly by raping and murdering one of the Koga clans daughters." She came across and put her hand on his shoulder, "We know you are sympathetic to this cause. And we will be very grateful".

Romeo started to feel all his meridians pumping and beating.

"Do not worry Mr Greene, that is what the herbal bathing does. It produces extra KI and numbs the nerve endings".

Romeo wasn't worried about the numbing, no he was worried about this so-called test. "Sounds more like a mission to me?" Romeo said letting his thoughts out freely.

"We need to be sure of your skills Mr Greene" He looked into the woman's eyes and for an instant he thought of Julie. "There is just one more thing Mr Greene."

He stopped thinking of Julie then came to a halt, "Yes?"

She whipped out a long sharp needle like a dagger and scratched him along the arm. He winced and she smiled. "The cure to the tiger poison Mr Greene."

He looked at the wound that had a strange warmth to it.

He kitted up with shuriken, Hanbo and Katana as well as various Metsubushi, potions and flash bombs and grappling grips. He gets down to the city and follows his keen honed senses around to the mansion that the opium merchant lived in. Two men stand on the wall smoking and joking with each other. Romeo scans around and listens. "Dogs barking," he thinks, they have obviously picked up his scent. One of the two men picks up his rifle and starts to do his rounds. Romeo starts to work the shadow skilfully watching for the guard. He hugs the shadow and blends into the dark just as the guard's footsteps get closer. Romeo moves closer waiting for the guard to round the corner. The guard walks by him Romeo moves closer slowing his breath and sliding a razor slim wire around his hands . He whips it around the man's neck and takes his head clean off. Then without a sound he quietly blends back into the shadows. The other guard suspects nothing and is stood looking over the ornamental pond. Romeo decides to scale the wall. He gets to the lip of the wall and waits to hear the guards breathing, putting a rhythm to it, a beat to the man's death. He hangs there a little longer trying to hear his heart, he counts the beats and he sends his senses reeling into the depths of nothing, then it happened he leapt striking at an ancient kill point on the guards' neck. Dragons touch he thought. Ninja have been known to wait for days for these points to become clear. Then they strike. Romeo looked around and saw the man's radio was still on, he switched it off.

Next moment he sneaked around the back of the modern building. A door opened and three men walked out.

"Shut those dogs up," said the first of the three.

"But I think they have got the scent of someone."

The first one who spoke smiled, "go on let them loose, I like it when they tear some would be up."

The other two men walked over and let the dogs out. Romeo slips into the shadows and heads straight for the pond. He crouches into the banks and waits. The dogs still smelling his scent come sniffing around the bank. They spot Romeo and start to walk closer. Romeo shows his hands and the three German Shepherds become very wary they start to snarl at Romeo and one gets too close. And with lightning-fast hands grabs the dog in front and splits its paws. Sending part of the leg bone through the dog's heart. The other two witnessing the viciousness of the ninja lose morale and begin whining and running. Romeo was instantly back in the shadows. His tabby's moving stealthily through the ornamental garden. The short grass telling little about the man's presence. The three men who had set the dogs free were now searching for the dogs killer around the pond. Romeo had seized the opportunity to enter through the door that the three guards had vacated. He gets in and pulls out a small internal map. He plots a course for the main study, where the opium merchant supposedly spends most of his time. He crosses through the hallway and comes to the study. His inner Ki goes mental and at this point he see's nothing, darkness.

CHAPTER 6

He is in his car riding home with Julie and the shopping. Then he feels a slap and is awake.

"Ahh our tiger striped friend is awake," The voice booms in his head as another slap is delivered to his face.

"He's only got one eye boss, it must be him."

Suddenly Romeo is face to face with what must be the side of a building. And sitting at a large oak desk is a short man with round glasses and slick black hair.

"You are a hard man to get hold of Mr Greene."

Romeo looked round and started to count, seven men including three of the snake Lin Qua that he had encountered in the city. He then looked at the small Chinese man.

"Who the fuck are you?"

The small man waved his hand and sighed. Then the large brick shithouse man slammed his massive fist into Romeo's face. Romeo's nose bled and the large man went to hit him again. But the Chinese man stopped him. Romeo looked up and started to fade in and out of consciousness. Then the large man threw a bucket of cold water over Romeo. He winced in shock Then immediately started to focus. He started to take inventory of what he might and might not have. Then realising that he had a throwing knife and various caltrops. He decides to make a bid for freedom. First thing he does is starts to circle his joints especially his shoulders, he does this using an old technique of ninjutsu yoga. And then begins to focus on the snake ninja as they appear to be his biggest threat. Meanwhile the Chinese man and his surrounding friends were having some sort of discussion on what to do with the Tiger striped ninja. The small Chinese man was meanwhile opening a small leather pouch in which were several syringes and a small bottle of pethidine, enough to kill a small elephant. He drew out a rather large dose enough to send the man reeling and talkative. He then ordered the Lin qua to hold his arms.

"This Mr Greene." as he drew closer flicking the bubbles in the barrel. "Is a serum from my motherland."

Romeo had by this time loosened the bonds near his feet. The man had begun to push the lance into Romeos arm. This was when Romeo struck he snapped his legs up and around the man's neck and snap! the vertebrae went on him. Then two of the snake ninja drew there weapons and tried to rush him. Romeo crouched into a cat stance. As the first snake ninja came at him rushing in to kill with his Sai aiming at Romeos neck, Romeo gripped the man's wrist and pulled the ninja off balance, whilst pushing his other finger into the man's windpipe crushing it. The second ninja struck and struck hard aiming his Sai at Romeos shoulder blade. Romeo rolled forward wincing as he tucked under and came up. He drew his knife and threw it at the Snake ninja who dodged and carried on in with his Sai. Meanwhile the ox of a man was sliding up behind Romeo. Romeo stepped forward engaging the other ninja in combat. They began to parry, punch, and grapple when the ox of a man rushed. Romeo sensed it and took the straight arm of the Lin Qua with his Sai and pushed it into the large ox of a man's heart. Romeo span out as he did this, grabbed the ninja's head and snap! The vertebrae went on him.

The remaining two ninja left before the melee had finished. Romeo gripped his shoulder and reached down for his hoodie which lay at the foot of the chair. He donned it and left the room and headed back to the Koga monastery.

He arrived entering through the exit used on missions. The geisha who had numbed him lay waiting in his room and one of them was ready to commit Hari Kirri. Romeo walked up to her and took the small tanto out her hand.

"It's over," He whispered. She collapsed into his arms sobbing, loss of face of this kind was particularly emotional especially when several ninja had already died trying to kill the opium merchant. This to the Geisha was bad enough, but to possibly set the two clans at war by using one of the Togakure ninja on a suicide mission, this was a total loss of face. She continued to sob on Romeos shoulder, this was when things became clear. The two ninja in America were sent deliberately to get Romeo over here their loss of face was serious. Their clan was on the brink of war with the Lin Qua. But it was far from over, the Lin Qua were plotting their revenge. But not on Romeo not personally. They were going for the old Shidoshi and they were prepared for a battle. Five hands and five feet were all it took. The head had been removed but the Chinese ninja body wasn't long in striking back, this time at the heart of the Koga clan. The Koga dojos. The first thing shocked and struck Romeo straight to his heart. The first attack was a low blow. A group of teenage students and they're sensei were finishing up when five foot attacked. They rushed in Katana and Kama's slashing and killing every-one in the room. The sensei was held and made to watch. Then his throat was slit. The bamboo mats were drenched in blood. It took the Koga and the families of the dead a week to clean it all. The eldest one was fourteen. The youngest nine. The Shidoshi's grandson Shuzi died fighting. He was the last to go down. And he took one with him. When the old Shidoshi saw this his tears mixed with the blood. But this was not the end of the attacks.

The red hooded ninja was walking towards the Koga dojo's. His name was Giro, he was half Japanese half Latin American. He was a large broad man who had been targeted by the Lin Qua's eyes the part of the ninja body that spied on these missions, Giro had sensed them the moment he left his house. This was all well, as now Giro's could take the ninjas to one of his grounds and fight them on his terms. It was time the Lin Qua learned why he donned the scarlet hood. He was big and knew one thing, he would do this for his favourite student Shuzi. But when he arrived at the area just off of a local garden he realised they had already went ahead. They had realised what the scarlet hood was for, they knew Giro was more than mere ninja. He was shinobi, the walkers of death. In the middle of the clearing lay his full ninja Gi including his Katana and Scarlet hood. This was going to be no picnic. In fact all ten of the ninja watched as Giro put on the Gi and armed the various pockets and sheaths. The foot and the hand of Lin Qua were told to take out Giro fairly, then they were to move on the old Shidoshi.

Giro knelt and started the tiger Kirri locking the fingers and saying the power words focusing in his mind on the trees surrounding the clearing. The snake ninja started to signal as the Kirri drew to zen the masters fingers gripped his fist. Then the first Lin Qua struck. But Giro had contemplated their moves, He had seen this coming. The first Lin Qua had swiftly crossed from the trees drawing his katana. Giros got into tiger stance. Then threw a crimson Shuken with deadly accuracy. But the Lin Qua had seen this coming and parried it away with his katana and kept coming. Just at the point of striking Giro, he rolled through and struck again with a second crimson Shuken, this one entered right up to the hilt in the snake ninjas shoulder blade. The ninja staggers back trying to pull the short blade out of his shoulder, Giro see's the ninja is off balance and rises quickly slicing the man's jugular. The Lin Qua's hand is next to strike. They move in and out of the tree's, silently and almost invisibly. Striking at the shinobi from the air and shadows. The shinobi starts to repel, carefully avoiding using up all his strength and letting his guard down. The number of them count more than ten. Thinks Giro. One of them gets to close and Giro takes his footing away and finishes him with a tanto blade in the chest. As he reaches back up several small, weighted Shuken fly at his head. He catches two with his left hand and ducks the other three. His skills honing more and more with the melee. He decides to chase the shadows. He slips the two weighted shuken into a secret pocket on his sleeve. Then slowly watches the corners of the trees for glints of light. He sees one and enters the trees instantly showing remarkable speed for a man of his size. He runs swiftly to a large tree in what appears to be the centre of the forest. He crouches, slowing his breathing and heart rate. Almost vanishing, he can still feel the Lin Qua's movements around him. He starts to finger knit again, to keep his pulses and energy flowing. The he hears it the soft landing of tabby's on the bracken floor next to him. He produces his tanto slowly and starts to circle the tree hoping to get the drop on him. But Giro's is on him taking his tanto and pushing it into the Lin Qua's left kidney killing him instantly.

He then swiftly moves again this time in the direction the Lin Qua came from. He spots two hand which are waiting in the trees. Giro takes out his climbing grips and climbs a tree adjacent to the two Lin Qua. He begins to slow his breathing again. This time projecting himself into two leaping strikes. He waits for them to signal to each other trying to remember the hand movements, knowing that they mean all clear. He then strikes suddenly. Leaping across and skewering the first from behind and holding him absolutely still so as not to warn the other Lin Qua. He then waits again for the other Lin Qua to signal and copies it perfectly, with the dead man's hand. Then strikes letting, the dead man fall to the ground and leaping again aiming his tanto at the other man's throat, He connects killing him instantly. He falls and Giro smiles under his hood, knowing he has killed the two signallers. He moves down the tree looking at the two bodies. Six more to go. The rest are foot. It's the last watcher he'll try to escape if he can. Try to kill the old Shidoshi himself. He spots two feet moving in and out of the trees 'bait' he thinks moving slowly around the clearing. Watching and honing his senses, He curses as he feels a sharp temperature drop he realises it's steel, a watcher part of the hand. He drops in front of Giro and Giro flips hearing the click of a pistol and a shot being aimed at him. He lands in a crouch and throws a Shuken at the man's midriff which takes the man down killing him instantly. He moves off counting the trees and marking them so as to come back to the watcher. So as he can come back and search through the Lin Qua's Items and look for clues as to what is happening to the Koga clan and why an ancient clan of Chinese assassins has come to wipe out the Koga. He starts to get closer to the two-foot Lin Qua. And suddenly he sees the trap that they have formed. Four men hide around a cluster of shrubs. The other two are waiting at the sides of the clearing. Giro pauses and thinks, waiting for the right move to come along. He turns and decides to challenge it head on. He strolls into the clearing with his master Katana drawn. He feels the hilt loose and brings out his tanto out of the hilt, the two Lin Qua at the sides rush at him. He does the Iron arm strike. And slices down one of their chests whilst he uses his tanto to strike the other man with the hilt of his tanto into his temple. He reels back waiting for the other four to attack. They come, launching Shuriken at Giro. Giro bats them away with his Katana as he pushes his Tanto into one of the other foots stomach. The four other draw there Katana's and attack. Giro takes the first two with quick razor-sharp slices as they charge with their Katana's aloft. The third and fourth slide in the shadows either side of Giro. Who positions his tanto and katana in a parrying position. Waiting for the last two foot who are circling either side of Giro. Who edges backwards into a larger clearing at the back. Hoping to gain a better advantage. He starts to breathe out. And settle into a slow rhythmic beat. Then the last two strike. He leaps over one of their heads and slips his katana backwards at the side of his hip. The Katana digs deep into the Lin Qua's back killing him. He then turns around and faces the last of the two. Who unloaded a Miriki Gusari. Which he begins to twirl. Keeping an eye on the Shinobis Katana which rest straight down his right shoulder Iron arm a technique which is passed down from shinobi to Shinobi.

The last Lin Qua aims one of the weighted end at giro's head. Which Giro dodges easily. He then rushes a sudden demon slice at the snake ninja's open guard. The Lin Qua quickly moves backward and tries to wrap the Mariki Gusari around the blade. Giro pulls the sword clear and draws it along the foot ninjas abdomen. He collapses to his knees gripping the wound and coughing blood. Giro Sheathes both his Katana and Tanto He then packs his stuff then removes his hood, all the while a tear on his face for SHUZI.

*

Romeo wakes with the Geisha lying across his chest. He listens quietly for the young girls breathing. He looks at her hair and starts to think of Julie. She stirs slightly and he smiles. Not bad, Not bad. She stirs again and he moves slightly to wake her but changes his mind. He drifts back to sleep. He starts to dream of the past, past lives, he dreams he is Samurai and sees himself chasing the young Geisha through fields of golden corn and catching her. They fall to the ground laughing. Then after they make love he looks up to the sky and starts to picture the two dragons unwrapping from each other and letting Julie go. He smiles in his pleasant slumber. Then all of a sudden they turn on the Geisha and begin to devour her. He wakes again this time clammy and short of breath.

He gets up and makes himself some Japanese green tea.

"Are you okay Romeo?" comes the young Geisha's voice.

Romeo takes the cup and sips, "Yeah I'm fine".

She looks at the tattoo's on Romeo's back. "A lot of pain, you have suffered Romeo".

Romeo smiled sadly. "Yes," he said turning the cup semi-circle.

"Tell me."

Romeo's head is bowed and a tear falls into the cup.

"No," he said with pain gripping his throat. He gets up and goes and gets some cereal and begins to eat. And think about things he has done the lives he has taken. He cries. Starts to sob. The young geisha crosses the room and cuddles the tattooed back of Romeo.

"Tell me?" she repeats.

"Okay." he says and starts to recount the tale of Sam and John.

*

Later that day when Romeo finishes about Sam and John he calls the old Shidoshi.

"Hello Mr Greene."

Romeo returns the courtesy, "Hello Shidoshi".

The Shidoshi sighs, "They killed Shuzi, Romeo."

Romeo's eyes sadden then widen in shock, "When?" asks Romeo.

"Last night, But it's okay Giro got payback last night."

Romeo smiled at the thought of Giro's the shinobi exacting his revenge.

"Shidoshi we need to talk."

The Shidoshi paused for a moment. "I'll be there the day after tomorrow."

Romeo placed the receiver down and smiled again. The old man was right, Giro's was a cold calculated killer, and would stop at nothing to get revenge, his methods were cold and bloody, he thought of the dream he just had and of the geisha. He placed the teacup down and headed back to the futon and lay next to the Geisha. She turned and rested her arm around Romeo's neck. He sighed and kissed her pale gentle hand. His left eye watering at the fact that he had fallen in love again. The sleep came softly and dreams that came were gentle. But deep in his heart he knew that this wouldn't last, as he held Julie to dearly.

He woke the next morning with a pain in his cauterised wound. The scratches he had made earlier were beginning to heal. She turned over as he shifted up from the futon. He sighed knowing that his feelings were growing for her in that single moment. She had become precious in the instance he had taken the Tanto out her hand. He looked at her hair and the naked curve on her shoulder. She was becoming vastly more and more precious. Romeo began to sob again.

*

He knew in his heart that the two dragons on his back would be after her soul. They bided it in his dreams, as they had taken Julie now they want her. Her? He thought of Julie, he thought of the pain those two men had caused Julie and had caused him. He watched his tears fall onto his cloth kimono. The pain and suffering, the stench of Sam Snide, the pain the aching in his anus, the coldness the... the... He sobbed as the pain reached his head, he began to think of what his therapist had said. The wild hate and mourning he had done over the loss of his child and wife. He began to sob even more the sobbing making his energy grow wild and wilder. He was turning feral. He was going deeper into the animal instinct, he started to growl then bang unconscious. And the young Geisha looked at her hands as the man silently slipped down onto the futon. She had stunned him, 'The last of the Koga Toxin,' she thought then started to check all of his pulses.

Romeo awoke two days later to the sound of the old Shidoshi's voice. He instantly relaxed and looked at the Geisha who was serving the old man tea.

"Hello Mr Greene, I see you are awake." The old man said this without looking at Romeo.

Romeo rose from his futon, and put on a cloth Kimono. The room was quiet and solemn. Romeo could feel the sadness in the old Shidoshi's heart. He crossed the room and knelt next to a small wooden table. And bowed as the young geisha placed a small cup of acrid Japanese tea in front of him. He turned the cup twice to the left and took a sip. The sour warm liquid warmed the tongue and bit the back of his throat. The Shidoshi sighed and looked at Romeo.

"Are you okay Mr Greene?"

Romeo took another sip from the teacup.

The old Shidoshi carried on, "I heard what happened to your wife and unborn son.

Romeo rested his small cup and began to focus on what Stephen had said. "Yes." the old Shidoshi whispered, "our problems may be more aligned than we think".

Romeo looked at the old Shidoshi solemnly, "yes Shidoshi".

The old man smiled, "You know they were our ninja that came through your window that night?"

"Yes Shidoshi."

The old man picked up the small cup again and took another sip. "We had no choice Mr Greene."

Romeo turned his cup again, "Shiddoshi, I have a feeling I know where you are going".

The Shidoshi smiled grimly, "Yes Mr Greene. But it is steeped in centuries of hate from the Chinese opium lords and there greedy cut throat Empire. The man that you finished three days ago was a descendant of a corrupt official whom besides running an opium slave empire also ran a sort of corrupt militia who delved into the black arts. They were accounted with the deaths of numerous officials as well as an ancient order of the monks the Shambala warriors. The few that escaped came to Japan and became the Yamabushi Monks who wandered the Hills",

Romeo envisioned these monks with their carved symbolised staffs and robes with large hemp ropes tying them. These ropes were often used as weapons of protection. Their spirituality was always pure and clean, as was their way. They chose their students carefully. Romeo smiled as the thought subsided. He noticed the old Shidoshi was watching him closely, scanning his features and looking at the content on Romeo's face.

"Ah Mr Greene your Sensai was right, you have met one. And obviously one of great distinction"

Romeo grew slightly at this, "Yes Shidoshi. Stephen had noticed this the day I stepped into his dojo".

The Shidoshi smiled and the sadness in the room lifted instantly. "Tell me of your meeting with Sensai Hayes?"

Romeo smiled at the memory. "Well Shidoshi, I had been going to a local Judo which had been only partially useful in easing the anger that was fuelling my energies. The Sensai had seen the rage would not subside. So he recommended the local ninjitsu club Togakure. The minute I entered I was fascinated. The students were grappling and a few were practicing with bokken. The Sensai on the other hand was kneeling practicing the strange finger knitting exercise, ketsu in. He rose looking at me and smiling, it was as if he knew me".

The Shidoshi smiled, "Saw you coming".

Romeo smiled in amazement as if the old man was seeing the whole scene in his head. Romeo continued with his encounter of the legendary Stephen Hayes.

After he told the story the old Shidoshi asked Romeo, "Have you had much trouble with your HIV?"

Romeo blinked at the old man and breathed in, "Yes".

The old man looked deep into the ninjas soul. "You know that we have certain herbs and toxins which boost the immune system."

Romeo stood up and walked over to the kitchen.

"Can I be frank Mr Greene?" Romeo reached into the fridge and took out a carton of orange juice. He started to gulp the juice down.

"You must marry my niece," Romeo finished his juice.

"Kinda figured that."

The Shidoshi smiled, "I know you are anxious for revenge Mr Greene".

Romeo looked at the old Shidoshi trying to figure out where the old man was coming from, "But the young Geisha you slept with, my niece is now infatuated with you".

Romeo's mind flipped back to the dream he had previously. "She would be better off without me."

The old Shidoshi poured himself some more tea. Romeo continued, "She may come up negative".

The Shidoshi smiled at Romeo.

"Besides," Romeo continued.. "I have bad luck with women".

The old Shidoshi smiled even more.

"She too saw you coming," Romeo looked at the Shidoshi in mute amazement.

"She loves you Mr Greene," Romeo half smiled. "She also saved your life."

Romeo was about to argue the point but the old Shidoshi continued, "In Japan we have a sacred rule, once you save a life, be it an animal you are ultimately responsible to it".

He took another sip and Romeo left the kitchen and knelt across from the frail old man, "I saved her life first," Romeo said looking into the man's eyes.

"My point exactly. Take her to the United States, you may find her a help rather than a hindrance."

The old man left the next day and Romeo sat next to the young Geisha and sighed, "I'll speak frankly to you." The geisha was glowing in her gown, her hair jet black and perfectly tied. "I'm dying of aids. My wife was murdered and raped".

She watched intently as Romeo carried on, "She was carrying my child. She screamed as the flames consumed her". Romeo looked at her solemnly, "The men who did these things to me will die".

She touched his hand.

"You must know that I will love you and that I have total torturous nightmares."

The Geisha pulled him gently from his speech and into her embrace and began to softly kiss him.

CHAPTER 7

John Carson and Sam Snide, were sitting in their cell with cigarettes lit. They had killed four inmates and scarred two guards and were top dogs in the Texan prison that they had been incarcerated.

The warden knew that no one would mess around whilst they two were up on top of the block. They had somehow been acquitted of the Malibu murders. And were doing time for possession of a large amount of narcotics and unlicensed weapons.

John looked at Sam, "It's time Sam, make the call".

Sam got up and walked over to the cell door. Then started to bang on the, and call the guard.

"Guard, guard, I've a call to make".

The guard walked up to the cell door and braced himself in case of the unexpected. He opened it up put his baton out as warning. Sam growled at him, and the guard felt fear running through his gut. All the guard could think of, was the last guard who had been two minutes late, and Sam had thrown him over the balcony. The guard and Sam walked slowly to the visiting room, where Sam started to dial a number. He spoke softly to the person on the other end then started to get angry.

"You'll just fucking do it."

The guard reached but it was too late. John Carson had somehow managed to follow Sam and the guard.

He gripped the guards head and swiftly bit the man's Adams apple out. The Guard fell gurgling and chocking on his own blood.

Sam grabbed the dead man's pistol and can of Mace. They headed through the visitors exit. Two guards tried to head them off but Sam was quicker, he shot the first one in the gut. The second one took a bullet in the chest which went right through the man's chest, laying a spray of blood from his heart and lungs all over the wall.

*

Romeo and the Geisha boarded the plane at Nagoya airport. The young Geisha was dressed in western jeans and a blouse, she had cut her hair and let it bounce lightly on her shoulders. Romeo was carrying her case which contained several vials of toxins and the dragon scroll of Iga. They strapped themselves into the seats and waited for the plane to lift off.

*

Sam and John headed round to one of their hideaways which was being lived in by several members of their chapter of hells angels. The men numbered seven. Unlocked the gates and let in the ambulance which they had stolen, killing its crew the minute they had heard their names on the scanner. The two men exited the ambulance and the biker they had left in charge embraced John. Sam walked straight into the building and went right into the war room. He looked at the wooden crates full of ammo and bullets. He looked around and found the crate that he had been looking for a single shot bazooka. He picked one up and snarled, "Fucking prison". He walked out of the room and signalled to three of the bikers who looked up at Sam, they could feel his anger and his rage. They knew he was mad at the prison. They grabbed their leather jackets as Sam headed for his Harley. The three of them gunned the engines of their Harley's. The gate opened and the four of them left.

John smiled showing his teeth, whispering to himself. "That's it Sam, stick it to them".

The biker who had embraced John walked into the building and went and got the angel dust which he had filtering for the last four days, expanding its pureness making it stronger, knowing that John would want it's strength at its maximum so as he could create hell on earth. In the room adjacent the war room the bikers had been testing their shit on local down and outs. Several of them had died and the rest were in a state of catatonia.

Every now and then one of the bodies was taken out of the room and out to the back yard where they were hosed down and then chopped up. The meat was then giving to the five large Rottweilers that prowled around the gardens. The angel took a wrap of the white angel dust and walked up to John and handed it to him. John racked up the gram into two lines then produced a small hollow glass tube and snorted the full gram in two toots.

He smiled as the powder rushed to his head and he started to see Sam as he rounded the corner next to the prison. The three angels dismounted and loaded their Kalashnikovs with forty round mags. Sam put the single shot rocket launcher on his shoulders and flipped the cross hairs and aimed at the guard's canteen. The police and some ambulance men were there. He fired at the guard's quarter and boom, it exploded. Meanwhile the three bikers began to gun down police officers and guards.

Sam joined in the carnage with a small automatic pistol. The body count got to over fifty before they stopped and headed back.

*

Romeo opens the door to his small darkly decorated apartment. The young geisha smiled at the smell of sandalwood and oriental musk.

"Bloom in the shadows," she said as she entered his sitting room. The rooms in the apartment were small but well lived in. She looked over into the corner and saw his scanner and ninja gear. Romeo put her suitcase into his bedroom. He walked through and sat down on his couch. The young geisha looked around the room then sat down next to him. Romeo lifted his phone and dialled Stephen. He let it ring and waited.

"Hello."

Romeo returned the greeting. "Sensei, I have the scroll and I also have some bad news."

Stephen arrived at his door two hours later. Romeo answered and let Stephen in. He spoke a few words in Japanese, a simple greeting and a curt bow. "I see you have a new lady friend."

Romeo looked at the young girl then forgot formalities.

"This is Kikieo," said Romeo. He then headed into his bedroom to get the scroll. Who's content he knew nothing about. The scroll was papered and brown with age. Stephen took the scroll and placed his forehead onto it. Romeo gazed on in wonder.

"Romeo they're out."

Romeo looked on in disgust.

"What do you mean they are out? How did they manage that?"

Stephen looked intently at Romeo. "They were put in general population, killed two guards and four inmates."

Romeo shocked and angry walked over to the window and looked out into the orange neon glow. He could see a couple walking into a stairway. He thought he saw a shadow and a flash of green but he dismissed it.

Stephen came across and stood next to him. "What happened over there?"

Romeo concentrated on the shadows seeing if he could see the flash of green.

"Lin Qua," Stephen looked out trying to gauge what Romeo was looking for.

"Lin Qua? You said, what were they doing in Japan?"

Romeo sighed, "I don't know, but I think they have followed us here."

Stephen looked further into the shadows. "Yes there is someone working the shadows" Romeo looked at Stephen suddenly. The Geisha walked through to the other room and started to look out her small arsenal. A tanto and several short dagger-like-shuken. She began to don her small grey Gi. That was given to her when she was fifteen and still fitted her ten years to the day.

Romeo heard his front door close as she left to go down onto the street. Stephen stood at the window the window and watched as she exited the stair. She began to work the shadows. Her grey suit giving very little away about her presence. Then she struck, the Lin Qua came out the shadows buckling under the pressure of several blows by the small Japanese woman. She appeared sending more blows his way. The man reeled and tried to gain some composure. He retaliated with some venom strikes to the Geisha, these are his best actions. Attacks straight back knowing that her best defence against a man like this is offence. The small tanto is produced during the melee and she strikes it under his armpit. Which pierces right through the man's lymphatics and up through his shoulder. Nearly taking his arm off. The man collapses and blood pumps out onto the road. She crouches back into the shadows and watches the man's last breath empty into mist into the air. Romeo and Stephen look on in stunned amazement.

Romeo sits down and watches the door frame for the young Geisha. Stephen continues, "Sam and John. Romeo, are you listening".

Romeo looks up at Stephen, "Sam and John have messed up this city for the last time".

Romeo looked on wondering "What do you mean?"

Stephen sighed "They blew up a building, not any old building but the prison they were in."

Romeo looked angry at this. "I was approached the other day by the police," Stephen said. "They have recruited all my black belts and all my spies to help in the capture or killing, these two men."

Romeo smiled, "They know about you Romeo. The detective Rolson he said that he knew you were under the arches trying to get a scent on these men".

Romeo stopped smiling. "What did he say?"

Stephen smiled knowing that Romeo was nervous. "He said that he found the bug that you placed into his car, and that was when he decided he needed us."

Romeo thought about this for a few seconds. "Does he know about the rapists in the van?"

Stephen patted him hard on the back. "Yes he does and he also understands why you did it." Romeo panicked then relaxed.

Stephen relaxed also, and as the Female Mata Hari went through the room. Romeo started to think to try and find a way to somehow get Sam and John. His first thought was Denny his tattoo artist. He put his feet up and fell into a deep sleep hoping he would wake the next morning.

He awoke the next morning to the smell of bacon and eggs cooking in his kitchen. His first thought of Sam and John and whether Denny had any leads. The Geisha smiled a she heard Romeo wake. She had spent most of the night watching his breathing. Checking that his REM's were running normally. Romeo watched her cooking. She still had on the top half of her ninja Gi. She walked over with the plate laden with eggs and bacon, tomatoes and French toast. Again, he smiled at this. He started at his breakfast slowly eating away thinking about all that had happened. He was trying to figure why the Chinese Ninja body were involved in this and whether they had some sort of link with the triangle. Whether they were connected with John Carson and Sam Snide. He carried on with his breakfast and chewed over the possibilities which surrounded the facts.

First encounter with the Lin Qua is when he arrived at the tiger dojos. He began to see that someone had twisted the whole thing to suit their own needs. He was beginning to feel who it was, who had the capabilities to set a trap with the Koga and the Lin Qua. Who had taught him the stealth secrets who had watched his progress bending them to their own needs. He dismissed the thought generally. He knew now who the string puller. He just had to wait patiently, take his time see how useful Stephen was.

Romeo finished his breakfast and sat pondering. Just chewing over the facts. The position he was in was one of honour, one of pain and fear. He knew if it came to the forefront too soon, he would be killed.

The geisha took his plate away from him and started to do the dishes. The sink was full he could see why the Japanese took pride in the work of their women. She believed in him more than he believed in himself. The man was falling more and more in love with her each minute, she suited the westernised clothing, the short haircut the place in itself enshrouded her.

The look of pureness stayed with her. The western world could never take away the spirit a Japanese lady. This would test Romeo's skills, he would need all his energies and skills, especially if what he just thought was true.

Stephen headed back to his home and dojo, and went straight to the phone. He dialled the number and over the other end was a voice in Mandarin.

"Yes Mr Hayes, we have a problem," Stephen smiled into the mouthpiece.

"Yes and No."

The conversation carried on for several minutes, but it didn't go unnoticed. Carl Rolson had already seen to the wire taps on both Stephens phone and also Romeo Green's phone. But this conversation interested the

Detective Rolson the most, according to the translator the two men were planning to trap Mr Greene and his new found love in a crossfire. In fact between Rolson's SWAT team and also the Hells angels that were under the control of John Carson and Sam Snide. Rolson listened to the interpreter who continued to describe a venue of meeting between the Sensai and the man on the other end of the phone.

CHAPTER 8

The venue was a small coffee shop just of the little Tokyo district in San Francisco. Stephen arrived early to avoid any unpleasantness. The Lin Qua, were very prompt and set boundaries on time especially when it came to business. And this was a particularly important meet as the situation between the Lin Qua and Romeo Green was becoming more and more dangerous. Stephen sat on a chair outside the small coffee shop, a small waitress with long dark hair and a short, chequered blue and white apron smiled at the man and asked him, "Coffee sir?"

Stephen pondered the question, "Yes I would like a latte. Colombian dark roasted beans".

The young waitress took the order down and went through to the kitchen.

The member of the Lin Qua appeared and sat next to Stephen.

"Okay Mr Hayes the where's and when's?" Stephen looked at the small Oriental man. "My people will set it up in the next three to four days."

Stephen starts to stir the coffee and watches it settle with dark bubbles on top.

"Has Romeo grown in strength since the trip to Japan?" The question settles into Stephens mind and he starts to consider the things that Romeo has seen and done.

"He obviously did something right over there yes?" Stephen rested on the question. Thinking he only took out your connection over there. "Well your men over there seem to have vanished." Stephen replied.

The member of the Lin Qua picked up a handful of sugar cubes and walked off saying. "Remember to inform the rest of the triangle before you make the arrangements."

Stephen sits there pondering over how he can do it. Then he finishes his coffee and heads back to his Dojo.

*

Romeo sits back after eating a dinner of Pork chops and fried eggs, 'good cooking' he thinks knowing his isn't up to scratch. The young Geisha smiles softly at him knowing that this is part of the Japanese Warm embrace. She begins to clear up the dishes, smiling sweetly and singing a small song in Japanese. Romeo listens intently, picking up the key words. He smiles knowing the song. It's about two love birds who save a Shoguns life. Suddenly the world seems lighter, he feels hope as the young Geisha draws to the end where the Shogun leaves them a gift.

Romeo and the Geisha bed down for the night. She lays there across the chest of Romeo listening to Romeo's heart and breathing.

"It's getting complicated," he whispers to her as he stares at the ceiling. He decides to get it of his chest. "I think Stephen is the third part of the triangle." The Geisha looks up into Romeo's face, "I know," she says silently.

Romeo blinks again then says, "We must prepare as now we are in the shadow of the sword."

*

Stephen waits outside the gates of the biker's den. He hears dogs barking as a large Angel with a small Heckler machine gun comes towards him, "Sam and John are busy".

Stephen looks at the man. "How busy?" he says back.

"Entertaining."

Stephen Smiles slightly, "When they're through tell them to phone me. The man turns around, his jacket showing the emblem of Bloodfang in the cold moonlight.

Stephen smiles "You do that, you do that," He whispers then walks quietly away.

*

Rolson sits at his desk looking at the pictures of the two men in question. Stephen Hayes catches his eye in particular. The look on his face is cold and still. Feelings seem to be cold and distant in the look he is holding. The other man, the small Chinese man. Rolson looks closer. He appears to be a lot colder as if Triad society had treated him colder and kinder at the same time. He knew this because of the way he was dressed, and the look of steel that he was throwing at Sensai Hayes.

Rolson decides to wait, taking time to chew over the facts. Sam Snide and John Carson are holding the city in a grip of fear. The triangle which the streets are speaking of is organising and controlling the trade of highly addictive narcotics. The fact that several homeless and a number of down and outs had vanished pricked Rolston's conscience, he felt as though his back was against the wall. Then there was Romeo, yes Mr Greene who had returned from Japan sporting a new lady. 'Romeo,' He thinks. 'The man is in so much trouble, in a game of deadly predators.' Rolson carries on chewing over the facts.

*

Romeo starts to gather up his kit, putting his Katana on top of his bag. He has a class tonight, it's Taijitsu. The young Geisha smiles whilst she puts away the dishes.

"You want to come?" Romeo says whilst laying his bag down at the side of the door.

She smiles at him, the paleness shining in the soft glow of the room's light.

"It's Taijitsu," She nods curtly and walks through to the room and then starts to gather up her Gi. She packs it slowly whilst thinking about Romeo's Sensai Stephen. She begins to see a trap being laid. Stephen is clever, thinks Kikieo, she gives Romeo a small kiss on the cheek. Romeo smiles and thinks 'The warmth will come stronger.

She smiles again, "I have a plan Romeo." The pawns were well played.

Stephen came up from a crouch and he heard the last part of the conversation. The Katana he held in his hand, flashed at the bamboo poles, four diamond cuts which take the poles of wood and bamboo apart. Then the sword sheathed itself in his hands. 'Yes Romeo, we have begun our last lesson'.

*

Romeo and Kikieo, head towards Stephens dojo's beginning the journey into the shadows. The kit bags rest on the back seats of the car. A still fear holds they're eyes onto the glistening tarmac of the road. The shadow of the sword becomes apparent in Romeo's mind. Kikieo's hand reaches across to Romeo's hand which is on the gear stick.

"You must temper your will, when you look the dragons in the eye" Romeo looked deeper into the shadows. He could see Stephen place the four cuts. The feeling of pleasure shone on his face. He had obviously been at the forefront of the triangle from the early stages. The Lin Qua were obviously his doing.

He had been turning Sam and John over in his mind. Tepo they would use, the fear of being shot had come forward every now and then. It was sullen in the car Kikieo had rested warmth slightly onto his left hand.

They arrived at the dojo where Stephen was warming up the class with Tiehen Jitsu. Break falls and rolls. The class seemed smaller than usual. Romeo looked around. Stephen decided to approach Romeo, Kikieo motioned him telling to guard his thoughts with techniques. Stephen stood before the tall man and short Mata Hari.

"Hello Romeo."

Romeo bowed then smiled, "Have you got any further forward with finding Sam and John?" Stephen smiled and puts his left hand forward to the young Mata Hari.

"Kikieo?" he says with a small sly grin on his face.

Romeo shocked, looks at the man.

Kikieo takes his left hand into hers. "How Sensai, how do you know my name?"

Stephen smiles, "Your uncle phoned me to say that your cousin Giro's is on his way over to help you out."

Kikieo smiles at Stephen thinking, 'he knows'.

Romeo blinks his eye. Stephen then steps closer.

Romeo looks at the man, Stephen then whispers in his ear "You have four days to return to Japan, then the trap closes."

Romeo looks deeper into his eyes and replies. "I will not bend to the will of your sword or your triangular trap".

"We'll see Romeo we'll see."

Kikieo looks at the iron trance which the two of them are holding. "Can we join the class Sensai?"

Stephen holds the grip of iron between the two for a second then answers, "Yes be my guests".

Giros has already arrived and is sat in a taxi so he can see the school adjacent to Stephens Togakure dojo. He too can see the look of iron and threats. He starts to unpack his Gi and weapons. The crimson hood lay flat in his hand. He has brought a black sash with him to cover the mouth of the hood. He knows now that Stephen is part of the triangle. So he must die at either his hand or Romeo's.

Romeo and Kikieo leave the Togakure Dojo. Romeo looks around knowing that the shadows will form as enemies, those who were once friends and fellow students are now his enemies. He sees a glint of red as he opens his car door. Then a sound of choking and the crushing of a windpipe. Kikieo smiles and touches his right hand.

"Giros has been here for many days now," she whispers lightly in his ear, Romeo puts his kit bag onto the back seat, he then takes Kikieo's bag and rests it next to his. The Koga and the Togakure were about to go head-to-head. Giros's red hood was a welcome sight.

"We shall see him later," Kikieo says as she sits down in the passenger seat of the car. Romeo smiles and starts the car.

CHAPTER 9

Stephen heads up to his flat above the dojo. He picks up the phone and dials the number of the bikers den. John Carson lifts the receiver, he has a young lady showering him with kisses to his neck and chest.

"Hello," he says gruffly into the receiver.

"Yeah John, its Stephen."

John pushes the lady away, "What do you want?" the question was harsh and brings a look of coldness to Stephen's face.

"You were suppose to have phoned me two days ago."

The answer to that was just as cold. And bit at John. He sat up his eyes filled with anger. A large rottweiler snarled as John threw it a look.

"Yeah I know, but like the man said I was busy entertaining."

Stephen keeps the look and hardens his tone. "Romeo knows and he has help."

John smiled, "Who?"

Stephen looks around seeing if he still has shadows and that none of them are moving.

"He has a couple young Koga ninja, There are good but not as good as my men."

John's face twists into a smile, "You mean not as good as my men".

Stephen's look of coldness is suddenly stopped as a large Bowie hunting knife is laid onto his throat. "Say hello to Sam, Sensai Hayes."

Stephen feels the coldness and razor edge of the blade. He tries to think of a way to take the blade off the man. But hears nothing not breath or heartbeat.

"Hello little pig," The large leather clad man whispers in his ear.

"Put him on," John says into his other ear. Stephen doesn't hesitate. He hands the phone over to Sam.

"Yeah John. do you want me to roast this little pig?" John grins from ear to ear.

"No man I need him, I need him, he is our connection to the far east."

Sam who still has the man with a hairsbreadth knife looks into Stephens eyes. "When do we lose this deadweight?"

John grins again. Stephens eyes widen with fear. He's aware that he is in the grip of the two most-cold bloodied and evil men in the country. Their gang are all ex special forces and the taking of life to meant nothing but the dripping of blood from the teeth on the back of their jackets, the bloodfang.

Sam puts the receiver down as the conversation ends and he removes the knife. In his other hand he has a small Heckler Scorpion. He points the sub-machine gun at Stephen and backs away out of the door. "Tut tut, little pig, don't even try for the hidden Shuken. I'll blow you away".

Stephen's face draws the iron look and cold steel is felt in his hand. Sam slips into the shadows, with the gun leaving last. Stephen relaxes with the Shuken in his hand. He's immediately starts to formulate a plan in which to lead John and Sam's gang against the Lin Qua.

*

Romeo smiles as he enters his house. He can feel Giro's, he can feel the man's presence in his small flat. He is knelt in front of Romeo's fireplace with several small Togakure arsenals. Kikieo smiles at him and Giro's gets on his feet. She then embraces him.

"Cousin," She says then smiles.

"Sister," he replies and a smile consumes his face. Romeo looks on in wonder.

"Ah Romeo the place fits you."

Romeo smiles and puts down his and Kikieo's kit bags. His sword rests quietly in its sheath.

Giro's points at the small arsenals which count four in total. "They were in the shadows and count four in total."

Romeo takes stock, seeing if he recognises any of their masters.

"Were there any Lin Qua?"

Smiling as he noticed a fifth dan's weapons, someone whom he had respected and hated. Giro's answers the question sullenly. "No there was no sign, not of their foot anyway."

Romeo smiles again thinking, 'They'll be next'.

Kikieo walks through the kitchen and starts to prepare, a small dinner of lamb and vegetables. Giro's kneels back down next to the weapons. Which valueless without their owners. He starts to take apart the flash bombs, and various other impact devices.

He produces a scroll and starts to write down the chemical in the powder and potions.

The air starts to fill with the smell of lamb and vegetables. Kikieo starts to look out the herbs and mint which she adds to the small cutlets which are simmering in their juices. Romeo begins to unpack his Gi and arsenal. Giros is still noting down the elements. Romeo crosses to the window and looks out onto the street. He is watching for eye's. The Lin Qua would be next to position itself in the way of Romeo's vengeance. Tomorrow he would go around to the dragons lair and see what Denny had picked up. He could see no danger from either the Lin Qua or the Togakure, but he knew it lay in wait, the shadows were cold but life and death was turning quicker and quicker on the streets.

They finish their meal and bed down silently for the night. The next morning Romeo wakes and hears a sound outside the door and rises. He lifts a pair of Kama, short sickle blades. He heads for the door, his tattoos rippling on his naked back. The Kama glint as the sun catch them, 'Yes,' he thinks, 'Someone has tried the door'. He curls down into shadow like a whisp of smoke. Giro's has also been alerted he looks at the clock, five thirty am it reads, he picks up his tanto and heads for the door.

The lock is clicking, Romeo makes a clicking noise in the exact timing as the lock. He begins to listen to the air trying to count breathing and heart beats. He stills his own heartbeat and hears two maybe three. His face blends into the shadows and his hands come into the light he grips his middle and second last finger so Giro's can see. Giro's gets the picture and readies himself. Romeo mimics the last click of the lock and smiles as the door begins to open. The first Lin Qua enters letting cool air in, he's unaware of the shadows at the doorway. He looks around with his Sai and Tanto which he holds in either hand. He looks at Romeo's bed and see's the small Mata Hari sleeping on her side. The second Lin Qua enters he has a Dadoa, he moves through quickly into the sitting room. He stands and looks at the empty futon. Still no movement from either Romeo or Giro's' The third Lin Qua enters producing a small pistol with silencer attached.

The three of them stand stock still. Kikieo has woken and produces a long slender knife. She rests waiting. 'A silent standoff' she thinks as Romeo curls further into the shadow, looking at the man with the pistol. He shortens his grip on the Kama and waits. Giros starts to count in his head as does Kikieo.

Romeo starts to direct his Ki waiting for it. The count gets to six and the Ki has begun to rise from his Hari. Preparing itself to leave. 'Seven, eight, nine,' Romeo's Ki leaves itself slowly and sharply. There's a click from the pistol and the Lin Qua's aim at the shadow that Romeo is in. The Kama goes forth into the light of the doorway. Romeo follows, the slice is quick and clean, taking the man's upper arm. The pistol drops to the ground and lets the shot off. Giro's is already upon the man with the Dadoa. Whilst the Lin Qua with the Sai has fallen upon Kikieo. Kikieo produces her razor fine knife and strikes straight at the ninjas throat which enters as doing so, she lets out a "hiss".

Giro's is dodging the scimitar like blade and striking out at the man's arms. Romeo follows through with his other Kama going for the man's head. The Kama connects across the man's eyes slicing sharply.

Giros meanwhile is fighting fast at the Lin Qua as his weapon strikes out fast. They are aimed at Giro's shoulders. Giro's moves quickly ducks under and slides his Tanto into the man's Hari. The sword slips from the Lin Qua's hands and rattle on the floor. Giros rises taking his tanto up through the man's belly and into his heart, the Ninjas eyes dilate and let the last of the light into his eyes. Romeo smiles at the steel handed ninja who is crouched on his knees griping the wound over his eyes. The blood is seeping through the man's fingers onto the floor. Romeo finishes him quickly. Puts his hands on either side of the man's head and twists, separating the spinal vertebrae. He gasps and falls limp. Giro's looks at the blood on the golden floorboards of Romeos apartment.

'So it has begun,' he thinks. Romeo hears the man's thoughts and answers out loud.

"Yes".

Kikieo pulls her long needle like dagger from the dead man's neck.

"Are you all okay?" She asks as she wipes the blood from of the dagger onto a rag. "Yes cousin" comes back the reply from Giro's.

CHAPTER 10

Stephen leaves his home and dojo and starts to head off to his meeting with the Triad. Rolson eye's the man through the lens of the camera. It's apparent what's going to happen next. The crossfire. Rolson clicks the camera and several pictures go through the frame.

"Mr Hayes it's nice to see and hear your true colours," he says out loud.

Then he begins to mull over the conversation between the Sensai and John. The Sensai's car leaves. Rolson has already traced the call back to the bikers lair. He knows if he and his team land too quick he'll lose position on the Triads. 'Romeo will win,' he thinks. There's someone else working with him. The four dead ninja that landed in the Mortuary were testament to that. Four Togakure black belts. Four of Stephens best.

Romeo leaves his flat heading for his Tattooist. Whom in a short conversation over the phone tells Romeo that he has the location of Sam and John. 'Giro's says he'll take care of the mess.'

Thought Romeo 'I must end the ring of hate and death, that Sam and John have awoken'.

He arrives at the Dragons Lair and Denny tells him to take his shirt off.

"Okay, where are they Denny?" He says as he takes of the shirt, and lays on the bench.

Denny looks at the red head and scales of the first dragon.

"I'll begin first," Replies Denny and starts up the gun. The first of the scratching is beginning to throb, the silence is defining in the room. A couple walk in and start to look around. Denny looks at them then then looks back down at his work.

"How many came at you last night Romeo?"

Romeo winced a little at both the question and the needle. "They came this morning," Denny carried on "were they Triads?"

Romeo turned his head and looked at one of his Katanas that rested on a wooden mount in the corner. "Yes Denny, they were triads."

Denny pulled the gun away as it caught in the power lead, "Thought so." He said gritting his teeth slightly. "You know your Sensai is in on it?"

The question made him sigh.

"I know," Romeo's eye under the patch twitched. "Where are they Denny?"

Denny laid the gun down, "I'll tell you Romeo, but you won't like who told me. And you won't like what's happening in that place."

Romeo relaxed as the endorphins settled into his skin and took the pain away, "why Denny, what's happening in that Den? And who gave you the location?"

Denny loaded a fresh needle and continues to colour the scales. People go in and don't come out!"

Romeo snarled at this, "What do you mean don't come out?"

"They are fed to the dogs."

Romeo turns over and looks at Denny, "What do you mean fed to the dogs?"

Denny looks into Romeo's eye. "Well I had a friend who walked by the back entrance. They were hosing down one of their victims whilst one of them chopped it up."

Romeo could feel the bile come up from his stomach and enter his mouth.

"The emblem on the back of their jackets is a set of fangs with blood dripping of them,"

Romeo sat up the bile still soured his taste buds. "How many times have they done this?"

Denny moved away taking the tray of inks over to the other side of the room. "Well the five Rottweilers are fed this at least once a week!"

Romeo could see the dog's feeding. Biting into the flesh of a corpse, growling, snarling. Romeo starts to shake the anger rising through his body. "What happens to the remains?"

Denny sits back next to Romeo. "They've dug a pit".

Romeo stands up tensing his back. "how many people are in this gang Denny?" Denny rises up and walks towards the Katana. Romeo feels the blood seeping through the ink on his back. "It must end and it must end soon Denny."

Denny smiles, "It was one of the Togakures students who gave me the location of their den".

He begins to scribble down the address on the back of one of his price lists. He then hands it to Romeo.

*

Giros lifts the last of the blood off of Romeo's floor his frame shadowing over the large stain. That had marked the wood. It had become apparent that there was much more to deal with than ninja. Romeo had told Kikieo of Sam Snide and John Carson. Kikieo started to explain the tale to Giro's. About how evil these two men are. Romeo arrived back his fists clenching as he stood in the hallway listening to Kikieo's version.

"It's worse than we thought," he said as Kikieo drew to the end of the story. "They have five attack dogs, that they feed on human flesh weekly."

Kikieo looks sharply at Romeo. The barbarism shocking the Mata Hari. "They also have enough munitions and weapons to take on the national guard".

Kikieo looks on at Romeo, "They need to come down, and they need to come down now".

Giros carries on after stopping to listen to Kikieo. The wire brush is lifting a lot of the stain, but the blood has seeped into the grain. Romeo looks onto the floor then at Giros. The bloodstain was lifting gradually.

*

The meeting had gone well with the triads. He decided that the triangle would close on both Romeo and the bloodfang. Rolson on the other hand would be placed elsewhere. So that Stephen could stand in the middle and watch. He would also put in place the last of his best black belts. 'Two days,' he thought. 'Two days and I know Romeo and the Mata Hari will be shadowing the den.'

Rolson takes down the whereabouts of the bikers den. The man who had phoned with the location said his name was Denny and that he was a friend of Romeo's.

'Romeo,' he thought, a trained killer with coldness and steel. It was obvious what Stephen intended to do.

The Triads were going to go into the lair whilst Romeo into the middle. The crossfire was imminent. "Two minds," he whispered at the piece of paper that held the location of the bloodfang. 'I'm in two minds whether you and your friends can handle this' The thought turned his mind sour. 'Romeo will start shadowing the den.' This eased the headache that had started to throb in his temples.

*

Romeo kneels a little off the bloodstain, and starts his Ketsu-in. His breathing slows down as he draws the first Kirri. He begins to look into to the den summoning the strength of the thunderbolt. Giros and Kikieo are in the bedroom doing the tiger Kirri meditation.

They have already been around and had a look at the bikers den. They spotted the main gates and the heavily built men with AK's. The focus and intent is on getting into the house. 'The dogs' They think in unison. 'The dogs will be first to die.' The Kirri breath moves through as their fingers lock. They start to follow through looking into the heart of the lair. They see the war room, then suddenly a fog clouds over their meditation. Then they see a large green snake then blink, their concentration breaks.

"We'll have company soon," Romeo whispers to them from the front room. "Stephen has matched us with ten of the best snake foot."

Giros rests his hands down on his thighs then speaks, "How do you know this?"

Romeo thinks on at the sounds he heard, "Whilst we watched I also listened".

Giros nods at this, Kikieo smiles. "I saw his intention long ago."

Romeo sighs deeply as Kikieo says this, "I wish it wasn't so Stephen, but you must die also".

The thought tinges Romeo's heart with sadness, he has memories of Stephen embracing him after his first grading. The two had been close and it hurt Romeo to feel this betrayed. 'Denny must have known' He thought. He turned around and looked at his back, The dragons were red and swollen at the ends of the tails.

*

Stephen sits up from his stomach crunches. The sweat is running down his brow, the tightness has shifted up his abdomen. He looks over at his kit bag and katana, to the left of the bag is a small red box. He had purchased the box two days previous inside it were two vials one had the pneumonia bug, super enhanced and put into a toxin. The other a form of E coli. Stephen smiles and turns over and starts to do press ups on his fingers.

He finishes and sits up and kneels. He can see his friend come off the plane. 'The last piece is coming into play'. He looks at the with his mind's eye. The tall lean man with shallow sunken features and cold staring eye's. 'Ghostlike' Stephen thinks to himself 'Perfect'. The man smiles as he wanders out the boarding lounge. His job was sullen. He had already heard about Romeos feats in Japan. 'The man had grown in strength' he thought, 'he must have really insulted Stephen'. The man liked this 'a move in power'. He picked up his leather case and moved towards the taxi rank.

Romeo gathered up his kit. He had decided that the Kama was his best choice of weapon. He also brought out his best Shuriken. They were silvery black with pin sharp points, and razor-sharp edges. He would need his chain mail gauntlets to handle these. Giros walks over to these weapons which lay in front of Romeo. The black cloth glitters with speckles of metal dust which had collected onto it.

The sharpness has cut the metal to a finesse. Romeo arms himself with the shuriken first placing them in small oiled sheathes. Giros watches patiently as Romeo does this.

"You are also shinobi," Romeo takes his chain mail finger across the curve of the Kama, sharpening it slightly.

"Yes," he says, "Windwalker".

Giros smiles at him, Kikieo enters with her grey Gi donned and masked. Giros looks at her with interest, he already knows her arsenal of short knives which she keeps hidden in several locations. Giros is next he walks into the room that Kikieo and he had been meditating.

Giros begins to undress, several small, lumped scars show themselves on his back and chest. Shuriken wounds from years of fighting. There is a small crimson tiger on his left shoulder blade, below it is another pale lumped scar. He starts to wrap his ankles in crimson then his wrists. The hood rests on the floor next to his tiger Gi. He begins to think of all the dead homeless people, how they are being fed to the dogs. Giros pulls the silk crimson sash around his waist, which covers a small bullet wound, His hands focus on the fold to the side turning the corner on it neatly. He folds it as he was taught when he was a young Sakura.

Romeo began to pull more breath out his Hari. Focusing on the several oiled sheaths. Romeo knew he'd have to be quick, as the walker in him was beginning to come forth. Sullenly he thought of the dead beggars and how the feeding frenzy would be wild on the starving dogs. Kikieo rests her hand on Romeo's shoulder.

Romeo looks up at her, "Shuzi," he says. the eye patch quivering as the muscle tenses with anger. The tear ducts on his long dead eye. Have salted slightly showing the wound pain.

Giros comes through his tiger Gi rippling with the binds and muscle. The pressure causing his meridians to beat and pump through the channels.

The man arrives at the Togakure dojo's. His tall thin frame looking up into the room which Stephen was in. He smiles and heads up the stairs. Stephen is knelt in the hall with the shadows at his back.

"Brian, your journey was comfortable?"

Brian smiles at the man. "I hear Romeo retrieved the dragons scroll!"

Stephen looked up then jumped onto his feet. "Yes two three days ago".

Brian open his suitcase and took out his kit. "The mission you have summoned me for?"

Stephen looked at the man. "Romeo has friends over from the Koga."

Brian's eyes narrow and he starts to note the shadows and light. "He is interfering with my trade negotiations with certain Chinese officials."

Brian smiles knowing that these are not just opiates.

"Meta amphetamines," Brian says to Stephen. Stephen looks at Brian's kit and notices the needle-sharp half knives. "I need you to finish Romeo, I have purchased two toxins which will finish him slowly."

Brian looked on, "I need him finished slowly as I know he and his friends will win the fight!"

Brian nods.

*

Romeo crouches round the corner his chain mail gauntlets shimmering coldness in the scimitar shaped moon. The Kama is slipped neatly through the tuck of his sash. He watches the two broad men as they stand there with their weapons slung. He calculates the movement, looking into the wind to make sure that the dogs haven't picked up his scent. Giros glints past the corner, sliding into a shadow. 'It's time' Thinks Romeo as he spots Kikieo scaling a fence at the other far corner. She lands softly. The night is dry with no breeze. Romeo draws his first Shuriken, it whistles gently then strikes the first man in the neck. He collapses the full metal object has embedded itself completely in the man's neck. The other see's this and hoist's his large calibre weapon. But nothing moves, not shadow or light. He moves over to his friend whose blood is pumping onto the concrete. He holds still looking again at the shadows. He begins to lift his weapon to raise an alarm. Blackness as the small Mata Hari's hands fall onto his head. The grip is tight as she separates the man's neck from his spinal column. She moves on drawing a short knife from one of her folds.

Giro's is next he is up and over the fence in two quick leaps and a grip. Romeo goes next, he slides up the fence, a slight scraping of metal as he reaches the top.

Romeo spots a dog eating at the remains of a corpse. The smell of decay and desecration hangs in the air. He produces another Shuriken and looks at the large black and brown dog. Another small whistle and the Shuriken embeds itself into the dogs neck. The dog whines then collapses. Giros crouches under a window and listens carefully. 'Music' he thinks, the sound is coming from further in the house. Romeo has rounded from the corpse of the dog he presses into the wall, avoiding the heat sensor which will light up the spotlight. The doorway is shaded and cool, he looks at the lock and waits, knowing that it's Kikieo who has the lock picks. He stands their listening, he also can hear music, the dull thump and whining guitar, and drums. The men inside are obviously having a party. Kikieo rounds the corner next, she has sprinkled the dogs water with scentless, tasteless arsenic.

"It'll hit them whilst they sleep," She says smiling under hood. Then she produces the lock picks. She eases the long serrated pick into the mortis lock. She then puts a small quarter pick next to it. Turning the thing slightly. It inches quietly the lock doesn't make a sound. Romeo feels the oak handle of the Kama, which is glinting like quick-silver in the moonlight. He decides to go forth. The door opens and Romeo slides through its shadow. The music continues to whine and Romeo can hear the panting moan of maybe two woman. Kikieo softly treads behind Romeo smiling under her grey hood. They move to each doorway, listening. Making sure that no one is coming through with weapons. They crouch at the last room where the music is playing, they can hear several men exchanging conversation, speaking gruffly. Romeo starts to remove the Kama from his sash. The small grey frame of Kikieo slips short half knife from out one of her folds. The weapon glimmers with a slight orange at the tip, envenomed with Kogas nerve toxin. The poison was a lethal instant toxin which in its ingredients was black lotus various other ancient ingredients.

Giros sets the count in their heads. Waiting outside the window with his Tanto and tiger clawed hand ready. The count gets to six and Romeo starts to slide the door open slowly. Giros taps the window gently and waits for it to be opened. Three men and a female vixen walk over to the window.

The door swings and Kikieo glances in as she signals to Romeo. 'How many?' Romeo signals back 'at least ten' The room is littered with drugs and empty beer cans. The music centre sits to the left of a three-piece sofa. Which is holding the frames of several men, with a hand full of women on top. Kikieo grips her fingers and signals the number eleven to Romeo, who is quick to signal back. 'we must be quick' He then summons the Tibetan thunderbolt one of the Kuji Kirris strongest action.

The vixen who rose at the tapping thinks it must be one of the guards having a breather. She opens the window and looks out. Giros strikes, gripping the woman's head and sending the Tanto through her throat. She gargles then falls back with the wound spitting blood as she lands.

One of the Bloodfang laughs and says, "OD".

Kikieo who by this time has produced a smoke device and throws it in the room. The men see the fuse and head straight for their weapons.

"Grenade," one shouts as the smoke bomb flashes then produces a large gas cloud. Romeo enters as the first of the women tries to leave coughing and spluttering. Romeo slices cleanly at her throat, sending blood across the room. Romeo knows where each person is and also that the window is covered by Giros. Kikieo slides through the door frame seeing the men reach for M.16 carbines, the small combat models.

The fuse of the smoke bomb has caused a small fire, with litter. Romeo smiles at this point he crosses through the smoke seeing the men point their weapons at both of him and her. He growls and leaps as they let they're weapons off at him. His Kama takes the first one's head off clean. And there is a large jet of blood that hits the ceiling and lands over the rest of the bikers. Kikieo looks up and see's the light bulb. She produces a weighted shuriken and blows the light leaving only that which is coming from the hall. Bikers begin to realise that they are out manned by professional assassins. People who are methodical and think before they strike. The bloodfang begins to lose morale, one heads for the window stepping on the corpse of the vixen. And trying to stretch with his legs out of the window. Giros takes razor sharp Tanto and wraps it in one swift movement around the man's ankle. He screams at the surge of pain, then there is silence as Giros rips his free hand with the tiger claw across the bikers neck.

The rest of the bikers are gagging as the smoke from both the fire and the bomb begins to choke them. Two of them fall to the floor asphyxiating and Romeo moves them sliding the razor-sharp Kama across their throats. Kikieo sees the other two who are heading towards the hallway with they're weapons firing into the smoke. She produces two Shuriken and launches them accurately at the bikers heads. They land dead on impact. Killing the two men instantly. Romeo smiles and looks at the fire that is burning well and growing bigger.

"Time to leave!" Romeo says then slips catlike out the door. Kikieo follows and they meet Giros outside.

The three of them watch as the place goes up in flames. Then disappear into the shadows as the sirens grow close. They don't realise but they have shadowed themselves and Brian intends to finish them as soon as possible. Hopefully while they sleep. Romeo and Kikieo rest after making love. Giros lays resting his eyelids counting the mystic symbols that are appearing in his mind's eye. He summons forth one of his Kuji Kiri and makes the mystic shape with his hands.

Then he sees him, the tall thin frame of Brian an assassin. The assassin appeared in the stairway slipping into the dim shadows that were held in the corners. Giros rises knowing that this man was no novice. He would need great skill to encounter the ghostlike ninja. Giros then thought 'he may even be Shinobi, and riding some sweet mystical poison'. Taking himself to the edge of oblivion then holding the fear and turning it into power. Giros slipped out and into a shadowy door frame. He waited, slowing his breath and pulling his Ki. The thin frame Brian sees the doorway where his victims lay and slips it's shadow practically unnoticed except for Giros who is watching the man from two points. His mind's eye and also his other five senses. Giros moves, agile with his naked torso rippling. Giro's strikes letting out a tiger like growl that catches the shinobi unaware. The strike impacts on the man's back and he winces then turns to face the large bull like frame of Giros. They begin to fight using gripping and striking techniques that are lightning fast. And thrown with deadly accuracy. Neither man can grip or strike properly at the other as their defensive techniques are evenly matched. Both using there Ki to its full potential.

Brian backs himself out of the doorway, His black Gi cracking as he blocks and grips onto another strike from Giros. Then the footwork their stances shrink into powerful half feet and catlike stances. They begin circle each striking and blocking as they turn on each other. Then Giros uses a foot strike and tries to stomp on Brian's foot as a holding technique. Brian see's through it and sweeps up and pushes his foot into the man's calf. Blocking it instantly there is a slight push from both men trying to free themselves from the simultaneous hold. Both hissing and breathing from their Hara's. Brian sees that it is a no-win situation and decides to take the easy way out. He pushes down the man's calf and produces an impact flash bomb, blinding Giros, so as he can make his exit out of the building. Giros who is still stunned makes his way back into the flat. Hoping that the man hadn't entered. Giros uses caution and checks the rooms. They now have a new enemy to face and he had a feeling that Romeo was the target. The silver half knives that the man never used but Giros had spotted. This vexed Giros puzzled him. Giros lay back down to rest keeping his keen senses on alert as the man may yet strike again.

*

Romeo woke the next morning to find Giros and Kikieo practicing in the sitting room. They were using Sai and Tanto's to fix out their strengths. Kikieo was winning, using her dark Tanto to very good use.

They were playing the arches in their feet, so as to strike quietly and quickly. The amount of times the young Geisha had struck the out at the large crimson stripped was too much to count, and all along in the melee Giros was telling Kikieo about the ninja in the hallway. She sighed and let her sweat drip of her and onto the floor.

Romeo produced a Hanbo and set a small challenge, "whoever can disarm gets the point and can use one of my Shuriken".

They stood facing each other in a triangle preparing themselves for combat. Then there was a swish and lunge, Both Kikieo and Giros struck. Romeo moved out the way and swinging his Hanbo to defend himself blocked the pair of them. Kikieo spun round aiming her Tanto for Romeo's neck. He parried the blow, then aimed the end of the Hanbo at her gut. She blocked the strike then kicked out with a powerful Mi Geri (Front kick). But Romeo moved out the way, Giros meanwhile was slipping up on Romeo trying to find a blind side but Romeo turned fast and struck Giros on the temple knocking him to the floor. "We had a visit last night" Giros said gaining composure from the blow. Meanwhile Kikieo was still trying to get past Romeo's Hanbo, It was crossing and turning in his hands, keeping a definite movement all the way in front of him.

They stood fast, knowing there was no way that they could get the wooden staff off of Romeo. Giros started to recount the action that had happened last night. And that the man was no mediocre ninja, he was highly adept and would most certainly be back.

Romeo slid into a pair of Jeans and white shirt, "I think I know who you are on about, and if Stephen has called him in, he won't be alone for long. The man is from England and extremely lethal."

Romeo smiled at Kikieo and she responded with a small bow. "Today I must hunt down, John Carson and Sam snide who will be making moves for another safe house".

Giros produced a small pistol about the size of his hand. "I'm coming too and I'm loading this weapon Tepo".

Kikieo dressed in a woollen jumper and cargo pants. "We're all going," She said slipping a wrist knife on. Romeo produced Kusarigama weighted chain and slid it down his leg.

Meanwhile the lone figure of Brian had hid out a few blocks away he was out his Gi and had on a muscle T-shirt and dark sun glasses. He watched as the three Ninja left the building and headed towards their car. They were going to the Dragons lair and ask Romeo's Tattooist the whereabouts of the two sociopaths.

CHAPTER 11

Rolson faced his office one more time and knew today was going to be difficult as he was about to be introduced to three special agents from the Asian task force. All the way from Hong Kong and Taiwan. It was such a mess, his city was ruined by the triangle. And seemingly most John Carson and Sam Snides Hells Angels. The bloodfang had been assassinated. Oriental style. Rolson was praying it wasn't a double cross or they would have both Triads and Chapters fighting in the street, a bloodbath. But Rolson was fairly sure he knew who it was. Romeo, Romeo the fake wind outside the bamboo hut. The storm that blew quiet and quick.

Rolson liked him and knew that things may yet go his way. The three agents stood there in Rolston's office quiet as can be. Rolson liked it that way.

"You men better be good?" he looked at the three young men. He sat down then said, "Name and Discipline?"

The first man came forward, a short and stocky With thick strong arms and red cracked knuckles. "Sam Lu Choy Lu fut".

Rolson had put in the requisition for the best and now he wanted to see. "Show me some?"

Sum Lu shortened and breathed out and showed him first the fingers of thread yet hard as steel. Then fist on the end of a rope. The man's upper body strength was tremendous and also his power was rushing the air all over the office.

The next man stepped forward, a tall man a six foot, lean with a small scar that reached under his chin.

"Name and discipline please?"

The man cracked out his arms and said, "Kim Sum and its eagle claw the 108 points of attack."

He began with two spinning kicks then straight into the claws aiming blows up the arms and on the chest. The movements stiffening. With the thumb coming into use.

The third man stepped forward, he was shorter than the rest and more lean, but something made him quick. In the way he moved and Rolson looked at his file.

And no wonder Wing Chun 'Yip Man Lineage' The man got right down to it, deceptive hands and showed his low kicks. He began to sound like a large cat growling more and more as he got faster. His punches were so fast, that Rolson missed them. They were the best the Asian Task Force had. He looked at their kit bags that were lying in the corner. He noticed the large butterfly knives on top of the Wing Chun officers bag and knew he was in charge.

"What's your name son?" The young oriental stopped warming down.

"Sam Ho," he replied and Rolson began to inform them of what he knew and what he expected to happen. The briefing went on for four hours. The men paid attention, It then got to the situation on what to do with Romeo, the conclusion was arrest him. Rolson wished it was another way but Romeo was wanted. The only reason he hadn't arrested Romeo. Was a morale thing.

He kind of hoped Romeo would win. But the three Orientals were giving strict orders that if they came into a fray they were to arrest Romeo and his accomplices at all costs.

*

Romeo arrived at his Tattoo studio. Knowing his source Denny had never let him down before. And this time he was sure Sam Snide and John Carson would be killed. He walked in and saw Denny sat there with his face black and blue and his eye pulped.

"They've been," He said raising his hand, the one he used for holding the tattoo gun. They had sliced of two of his fingers and his thumb. The wounds were stitched but his ink days were over and he knew it. He smiled at Romeo through his missing teeth and said, "This won't shut me up".

Romeo looked round the trashed studio and said, "Who was it Denny?"

"Well it wasn't John and Sam. It was your Sensai. Hayes."

Romeo sighed and went on, "Well just as well it wasn't them you would be dead".

Denny took some solace in the fact that it wasn't they two, and the fact they had left him alive was a big mistake. As he knew the location of the bloodfang. And John and Sam. One of their chapter had turned yellow and gave Denny there location. The Hells angel had also spilled his guts on how they had tripled the guards, And that Sensai Hayes had sent a couple of ninja in to watch the shadow play. The ninjas had seen the carnage of the last attack and made a good vantage point of the outer perimeter of the large brick mansion. The rottweilers were taken inside and they expected an assault at any time. Sam snorted his PCP red devil angel dust. It was like a hundred tabs of acid but faster working. John was petting the dog that was left and said "Satan." "Show me your teeth!" The dog growled and bared the right side of its mouth showing it's fangs.

Romeo helped Denny tidy up and decided he must end this rivalry with Stephen, he looked again around the studio and let out another sigh.

"Such a waste to happen to someone so talented," He muttered as he began to clear up.

*

Night was drawing near and Romeo was readying himself by donning his black Gi. Kikieo donned her grey Gi and Giros put on his black suit with the crimson hood.

They armed themselves without even noticing the shadow of Brian, watching through the windows.

But someone else had noticed and that was the three special police from Hong Kong. And they knew that this was a showdown. Romeo left the place quietly, first sliding into the shadows and running on the balls of his feet. Brian saw him and instantly followed he too was on the balls of his feet. And donned in black, Giros went next crossing over the road and sliding into the black alley. Romeo felt he was being watched and followed and slipped quickly into another shadow and waited.

Kikieo slipped out next and followed Giros. Hiding well in the dark alleyway running fast and silent, her Tabi's leaving no trace of her whereabouts. Romeo waited just off the alleyway and saw the Ninja. The lean figure passed by his hiding area. And carried on to Stephen's dojo. Romeo smiled then he saw the car and three Orientals in heavy canvas wu-shu suits. He wondered whether they were triads or not.

The three ninja arrived at the Togakure Dojo and began to flip and slide into the shadows. They would have to be quick in their attacks as they were heavily outnumbered by Stephens lot. Romeo unsheathed his Kama and made for the centre of the class which was a seniors seminar. Giros produced a pair of Sai and pushed them in the air in a crossed show of strength. Stephen bowed and said in English, "This battle was always going to be. The Tiger versus the Dragon. All seniors must know that this is no test and that Romeo is here for his honour."

The class began to produce weapons. Shuriken, Tonfa, Katana and various other weapons. Kikieo produced a blow pipe and crouched into the corner like a phantom statue. Giros moved to the centre of the room and the class began to circle Romeo and Giro's. Stephen struck first and struck fast. Kikieo produced a small bamboo pipe, and crouched into the corner, invisible silent extremely deadly. Giros moved to the centre of the room whist Romeo faced Stephen. The seniors started to circle Giro's, And it began Stephen sliced down at Romeo as he leapt through the air.

Romeo parried and struck back with his weapons of choice, Kama. Taken the razor-sharp scythe blade across His old sensei's chest. Meanwhile Kikieo began to fire off little darts with a deadly poison that caused instant cardiac arrest. They were going down with instant loss of breath. It was called a sudden cardiac seizure.

Giros was parrying and striking at the rest of them. There numbers were growing short. Giros had mortally wounded three of them and managed to dodge Shuriken of another three of them. Romeo was embroiled in a deadly match of parry and strike. Then as if they were tuned into each other they switched each other and faced each, others enemies. This really surprised Stephen as he was expecting to finish off Romeo, but Giros was really quick and pushed the blade of one of his Sai into Stephen's chest the other through his throat. He gargled viscous red liquid then as Giros pulled the Sai free he crumpled with a sickening crunch.

Giro's stared into Stephens eyes as the lights went dim in them. "That's for Shuzi," he hissed as the man clutched at the wound through his throat. The rest began to circle Romeo, Romeo crouched into the perfect Tiger stance with both of his Kama facing east. Giros leapt and began to push his back against Romeo's Back. Kikieo did a forward roll into a standing position throwing a small razor-sharp dirk at the heaviest set of the three. It made a splash of red on the wall at the rear of the Ninja as said weapon went straight through the man's neck. The mats were drenched in blood.

*

Carl Rolson, headed off with the Hong Kong task force. They arrived at the scene of the carnage. But Romeo, Giros and Kikieo, had departed. They were on their way home. When they drove past Rolson and the three Chinese men. They got round to the apartment and headed up to the flat. And then bedded down for the night. Carl Rolson was speaking to the head of forensics.

"So Stan?" said Carl. "What's the damage?"

"Well they won," Said the man with the camera.

"They won?" questioned Carl, who was feeling the heat of the arising problem like a dull ache in the back of his neck.

Then Stan began to give a blow-by-blow recount of the bloodbath.

"Who did the most damage?" asked Carl.

Stan smiled and pointed to the corner that had housed Kikieo. "The lady with the blow pipe, she took out close to a dozen of the men. She didn't even sustain a scratch."

Carl was impressed by this and said, "What kind of poison did she use?"

Stan took another picture and replied, "It's exotic probably nerve inducing. Worked instantly, they didn't stand a chance."

Carl huffed and looked around, "none of them did". He said, as he continued to look around.

Carl introduced the three Chinese men to Stan. Stan shook hands and bowed to each, he was impressed by the three Asian task men. They looked like serious hombres. The physique on each was impressive each one of them looked like they had been. Forging their bodies in the studious and physical fires. They each had a certain glint to them. They were trained and trained hard. Probably since early child hood. Carl motioned for the three ATF men to follow him. Then they headed in the direction of Denny's tattoo parlour. They were going there because of a few loose ends that needed clearing up.

*

Brian watched as they drove away, mentally noting the three men watching for characteristics on each man see what sort of discipline they had been trained in. He guessed each one right to the area and its major discipline. He got the Wing Chun guys straight away. He was more with an air arrogance. Almost feminine. It was that fact that gave up his style, as he knew that Wing Chun was invented by a Buddhist Nun (or Oni) as they were called. She was the reason the Wing Chun Knives were called butterfly Knives.

Brian sat adjacent the tattoo parlour whilst. Carl went in to the Dragon's den and the three ATF stayed in the car. The other two the short wide-framed one he got next. Choy lu fut. Of the south China fist. The eagle style he got next. He could see the man tensing and relaxing his finger. not cracking but bending them in his hand. Each finger wiry and strong like steel. He was the dangerous one. He could paralyse, cause severe pain even kill with those fingers.

The right grip at the right time could cause severe pain, blindness instant death. He was going to be a deadly opponent. Brian watched as they sat. Carl who was in the parlour of Denny. started to have a heated discussion about the law and who was responsible for taking care of said laws. Denny as it turned out had been a very good informant to Carl. But this time he was going to pass up on the information trade, no in fact he was swearing on his families souls that he had nothing. Carl was getting ratty to say the least.

Brian gunned the engine of said muscle motor and drove away. One of the Orientals, the wing chun expert noticed said motor driving passed and said the licence plate out loud, making a mental note of it whilst he said the number, the agent of the South China fist (Choy Lu Fut) wrote it down in a pad. Just in case.

"What do you know about an outsider?" Denny sat down and said, "fuck it".

Then Carl crossed over to the window adjacent the street. "His name is Brian MacArthur. He is a ghost, very few people have seen him in the flesh. And the majority of them died."

Carl smiled a small sensible smile and said "Well thank you Denny".

Denny looked at what was left of his hand. "They have moved, the Angels, they have moved!" Denny looked at the Detective. "I don't know where but I'll get word soon."

Carl smiled again, "And Detective," he continued. "Stay out of Romeo's way."

Carl opened the door and made his exit. "If it's a fair fight and I think Romeo could lose then I'll intervene, But the Triads are involved."

Denny Scoffed, "Romeo eats Triads for breakfast".

"Trust me Carl stay out the road". Carl walked through the rain that had suddenly started he pulled the collar up around his neck and walked to the car.

*

Romeo produced his Kama and in proper ceremony he cleaned the blades, letting go of all the souls that had been taken by said pair of blades. He then at the end of the finger knitting Gave a small Kia. That was meant to seal their spirits in Hell. The blades were now blessed.

Kikieo produced a set of Shuken, stars of her clan were rare to find. So she kept reminding herself that they were a gift from the gods of her homeland. She poised in true Shinobi spirit and threw two at a time splitting from each other and landing in the two bamboo posts that were wrapped in tight hemp rope. They arced and gave off a little thump at the exact same time. She was very adept with missiles as you might expect from a Koga Ninja. Romeo hung the Kama in their sheaths behind the closet in his bed room. Giro's began to sharpen his Sai.

"I think it's time to have a standoff." Said Romeo looked at the two Ninja. He couldn't hand pick a better pair of Ninja. No, not in a hundred years. Now to the matter of the Lin Qua. How he would make it plain to the Chinese Assassins that they were through.

He sent a messenger to the Chinese underworld. 'We wish to meet for a final stand-off, We are wanting our honour satisfied'. The Chinese courier wrote the note. 'You must realise by now that I have already dispatched my old traitor of a Sensai Hayes, And if you wish you may contact the Hells Angels and have them join you in this stand-off. Yours honourably Romeo Greene'

The teenage boy finished writing then off he went to the Triads biggest gambling den. "Will I secure the reply before I leave?" asked the young teenage oriental. Romeo nodded then bowed. The youth rode quickly away and onto an old dirt bike.

CHAPTER 12

John and Sam were drinking and doing all the drugs under the sun. They may have even participated in cannibalism. Well, they had dug two mass graves already. And the homeless problem was disappearing gradually. I mean they were cooking, smoking and drinking. They had a major shipment of heroin coming from Thailand. They were also waiting for the go ahead on a full up-front assault on the three ninja. But the Lin Qua were wanting justice on their terms. And that was a cold motherfucking fact.

But John and Sam had made a tonne of cash enough for them to retire. But that was a whole world away. A different challenge. A new dawning for the two bikers. But first the grin spread across John's Face.

"Romeo," he said and pushed the magazine clip into his black dessert eagle firearm. With very little force he slid a bullet into the chamber. He then aimed at one of his crew and blew the fuckers head off.

"Next time one of you fuck up I kill you all. You got that motherfuckers?"

He then emptied the rest of the clip into his Bitch, a fine lean blonde, with tits. Well they were pretty fucked up after he shot her eight times, each bullet ripping through the girl leaving arterial spray all over the guy's mate. The girl lay on the floor bleeding from exit and entrance wounds.

"And that's for my dogs, You'all got that?"

Her body twitched as the last of her blood pumped out of the wounds. He then shouted for someone to clean up.

*

Romeo sat in Do position which was comfortable and welcome for a change. The door was softly rapped by the young Oriental teenager.

"Enter" he said softly and the young man heard and responded by gently pushing the door open before stepping cautiously into the house.

Romeo smiled and continued, "what news from our Snake headed friends?"

The young boy smiled and replied, "They were very curt, and offensive. They said that the loss of face was not theirs to adhere to and that they wish to bow out of an all-out war."

Romeo let out a strong sigh, part relieved part curiosity, "what, they don't want a fight?" asked Romeo.

"They sir, have no affiliation to the two bikers and wish to bow out of said carnage."

Romeo stood up at this point and said, "Their honour is just as damaged as is mine and my two friends. They wiped out nearly a full clan of Ninja in Japan. And I was there first hand at said carnage. Tell them, no sir, they don't have the option of bowing out we end this now".

The young man bowed and headed back to the Lin Qua. Knowing full well they may shoot said messenger.

Romeo smiled as the little engine of the dirt bike tore away to China town. He gathered his kit together and made fresh wraps for his hands and feet. Then gathered his razor sharp Shuken and Kama. He also loaded up on impact flash bombs. Whilst Kikieo finished her Kanji with Tepo (Firearms). Giros slid his Katana into the sheath on his back. His crimson hood. Was donned last. Romeo covered his bad eye and also put on his hood last. Then on went the chain mail gauntlets. Kikieo tied her hood and slipped her small calibre pistol that had three shots in it, into one of the pockets in her Gi. They just had to wait now for the messenger to get back to them.

They waited for about an hour, then as the night was drawing near they heard the engine of the dirt bike travelling towards them.

"Here we go," said Romeo, hearing the engine come to a halt, at the bottom of the stairwell. The messenger strode up the stairs to Romeo's front door, he rapped the door gently again and again waited for Romeo's voice to ask him to enter. He pushed the door open and instantly bowed when he saw the dark shadowy figure of Romeo.

"They will meet you in the warehouse area just south of Chinatown. Two hours."

Romeo smiled under his hood. "Okay," he said and handed three grand to the young boy. "You did good Li," He continued.

The young oriental smiled, bowed then walked away. He kick-started the dirt bike and headed back to his real job delivering Chinese meals.

*

Brian MacArthur sat adjacent the flats, and noted the young man's coming and going's. You didn't need to be a genius to know it was the prelude to a battle. But where was the battle, he would have to follow the three Ninja and try not to get noticed. He waited. The three ninja came down the stair like a shadowy bad dream. They got into their dilapidated car, which had seen better days. And drove off to the Warehouse district just south of Chinatown. Brian tailed them with a degree of skill which could only be done by experience. No he was an expert a true skilled technician of the highest degree. The three ninja had no way of knowing they were being followed.

Carl stopped his car outside the Golden Dragon takeaway. He whistled at one of the delivery drivers, and shouted, "Where's Li?"

The man rolled his eyes and thought 'Fucking Cops'. The man turned around and beckoned the detective to come and talk. Carl turned and looked at the three ATF and said, "You want anything?" The Young Wing Chun Expert smiled politely and replied, "no thanks".

The detective looked the man in the eyes and said, "You know if this lead checks out, you three may get home early".

He then got out the car and went over to the young Oriental. "Li is on a delivery. He should get back in the next half an hour. You wish to wait?"

Carl smirked and said, "We'll wait," Carl laughed a little and said. "I'll have an egg roll and a portion of spicy ribs".

Five minutes into the meal, and Li arrived. Carl wiped his hands clean on a napkin and exited the car.

"Li? Hey Li." Then he put his hand on the young man's shoulder.

The young Oriental turned around and said. "How can I help officer?"

Co-operative thought Carl. "Where is Romeo? And where is his next assault gonna be?"

Li smiled, "Am a poor Chinese boy. I only deliver food."

Carl laughed then gripped the you lithe Oriental, and pushed his wrist. Then slammed Li up against a car. He then began to pat him down. Finding the three thousand dollars in his pocket. "Poor Chinese boy, huh what's this?"

Li just grinned at the detective.

"That's my college money."

Carl looked and nodded at the youth. "Yeah, yeah, yeah."

He said, "Then you won't mind picking it up at the station" .

Li smiled as the hand cuffs were taken off. "Tell me where Romeo intends to strike next and I'll give you the golden treatment."

Li smiled and rubbed his wrists back to normal. "And what is the golden treatment?"

Carl grinned and then continued, "I will double that roll of money for one".

Li smiled and said, "And?"

Carl handed back the money and said, "If you are ever in trouble I will personally see to it that you are set free".

Li shook his head and then told Carl Rolson the details concerning Romeo, Giro's and Kikieo. He smiled as the young man spilt the beans. He stood there knowing that time was a factor in this, so soon as Li finished. He walked to the car. They were 10 minutes away, but Rolson was adept in working his car. He was the best offensive driver on the force. When he was younger he had the best record for catching DUI's he spun the wheel around doing a perfect doughnut. And screeched of while the cherry spun a red light into the night.

The three Oriental's seemed not a bit afraid as they bit the bullet. The short ATF agent patted Carl's back and cheered him on. "I told you he weren't a sissy Gwai Lo," he said to the other two. The car was speeding at nearly eighty miles an hour on the highway. They all had huge grins on their faces. Except for Rolson whose eyes seemed to go red and he wore an evil grimace. He looked almost Satanic, evil, he then as soon as they hit closer to the meeting point, he stepped harder on the accelerator, and spun into the warehouse district. Then he stopped on a dime and switched the engine off. Then sat and calmed himself down. They waited knowing Romeo would either be on his way or somewhere close by. They sat very still and watched as the shadows began to grow. Then flip. A shadow flew across from them. They began to feel the fight starting.

*

Romeo exited his car whilst Giros and Kikieo came at his rear. Giros smiled as he could see movement in the shady parts of the buildings. The eaves and awnings of the buildings seemed to grow then fade as the three ninja moved further into the district. Move without trace, it was old martial arts magic. Only those of great experience, could move and keep hidden with such skill. Giros was a master at spotting said technique. And totally prepared for the onslaught. Kikieo vanished from sight slipping gently into the shadows. There was a little hissing then the cat like growl as she fended off four or five Snake Lin Qua. Two of the five had been dealt silent and deadly strikes with her using her Shuken as hand held knives, the poison on said stars acting extremely fast as it was the same toxin she used on her darts for the blow pipe. She carried on fighting the other three when one was felled by one of Romeo's self-sharpening shuriken. It went straight through the snake ninjas chest and came out the back of the man. Giros on the other hand was fending himself deliberately as if he was wounded. This was to gather how strong their force was. He knew they would try and rush him with as many they could. Going in for the kill. Giros slipped intentionally. He lay playing dead. And began to watch through his eyelids what was going on, counting movement. He had used this technique a few times and every time he had successfully completed said missions.

The battle began to heat up as they travelled deeper into the district. Giros lay dead and carried on counting as his two friends fought their way into the heart of the area. That's when Giros counted twenty or so Lin Qua, then something caught the corner of his eye four men leaving a car slightly to the east of his peripheral vision. It was the cop that Romeo had told him was heading up the investigation. And it appeared to him that he had three Oriental friends. Now this was interesting,

"A small but deadly task force," He said. He had been tracked by similar agents before but had always found them to be useless. He usually played cat and mouse with them then ditched them whilst they were truly confused and baffled. Giros liked the way this was heading.

"The more the merrier," he said then flipped onto his feet. He continued to watch as the four of them walked closer to Romeo and Kikieo. Who were having the fight of their lives, There were at least twelve of the Lin Qua circling Romeo and Kikieo. And that didn't even include the dead that Romeo and Kikieo had sent into the fiery pits. It was at least seven each. Then the game-changer happened.

Brian MacArthur appeared. He took two swipes at Romeo then vanished. Romeo had felt the assault as it was being served to him and had used his Kama to great effect. Blocking said swipes sending a huge shrill as Brian's half knives came into contact with Romeo's Kama. Then gone. He wasn't called 'Ghostlike' for nothing. Romeo began to remember the stories he had heard about Brian. The man was a legend. He was known for his great skill over vast problems. Things that only he knew. As he didn't work with others he was the true guerrilla. The true lone Tiger. Romeo hoped that Giros was fast behind Kikieo and himself. But Giros was watching as the four Policemen charged into the rear of the hostiles that were bearing down on Romeo and Kikieo. Rolson began to skip from foot to foot. The three ATF went straight into a cluster of them. Seven or more. Rolson began to jab and cross at one of the Lin Qua.

Then the three A.T.F went back-to-back and began to block, parry and strike. Fast inch punches were hitting into the Lin Qua. And with deadly accuracy, were sending their opponents flying. Rolson was jab, jab hook cross. And smashing his burly fist into the black covered Chinaman, smashing his face to pulp. He kept momentum up and delivered several more Jabs and hooks. The man after several more of the powerful Jabs hitting, stopped suddenly and collapsed. The severity of the wounds finishing him for good. The South China fist expert. Was duelling to the death. His fists covered in blood. His breathing regular with no scream or noise at all. He was landing blows to three different Lin Qua. Whilst the eagle claw was stunning two or three of them and then going in for a heart stopping Eagle grip. At the one that was getting the best of Romeo. He flipped over the statues of the three Lin Qua who were soon to die as the blood would stop pumping in their veins. And they would fall down dead. The Wing Chun ATF agent was parrying and aiming short half inch punches that were sending his opponents flying then the pressure of his blows were causing the Snake heads hearts to implode.

Giros came round the left side knowing Kikieo was having a bit of trouble fighting the three Lin Qua that were left. Giros produced an envenomed blade from one of his pockets threw the weapon at the one that was causing Kikieo the most trouble. The blade landed right in the side of the Snake heads neck. He gargled his blood and fell down dead. The other two were still hard at combat with Kikieo, and they knew from experience that the young Mati Hari was not to be underestimated. She leapt at one of them giving off a Mia Geri (Front Kick) Smashing the man's face. And putting him out of action Giros went swinging and stabbing his Sai.

Using a cross block at first. To stop the knife of the Lin Qua. Then he pulled one on the Sai free and stabbed through the man's lung killing him instantly. Giros pulled his Sai free and the man fell pumping blood all over the wet pavement. Carl was still going toe to toe with one of the Lin Qua, he was bobbing and weaving. Every now and then throwing a dummy punch that took the Lin Qua by surprise. Then hammering his opponent with Jabs and uppercuts. Beating them to death with kidney punches and straight-out punches to the men's face's. He was totally in charge.

Romeo began to look around for traces of the ghostlike MacArthur But saw no one. He then heard the engine of an expensive small sports car. Revving and in full throttle. It shot out the warehouse district and headed back to his hotel. Romeo began to curse in Japanese, "Backai, Backai" He then looked at the carnage around him and thought 'Just two more to go. Then I will leave this world in peace'.

He wandered up to Carl who was wiping the blood of his knuckles. He lit a cigarette inhaled letting his lungs fill with smoke and said ,"That was a pleasure cruise". Romeo put his hand out to shake and be polite.

Carl gripped his hand and said, "See I was a Marine Boy a few years before your time. And undefeated boxing champion in the Navy. Even seals respected me. They couldn't keep up with me in and out the ring".

Romeo smiled under his hood and said, "You certainly don't pull your punches, unless you are beguiling them throwing feints and dodges".

Carl smiled,. "Hi am Carl".

Romeo looked at the mans rugged jawline and said, "I'm Romeo. Thank you for your intervention."

Carl laughed throaty and deep. "I know you," he said.

"Yes you're the bum out in the Malibu estate," Romeo had been made.

He smiled and removed his hood. The blonde hair falling just short of his bad eye. Kikieo came over smiled, removed her hood and said, "I'm Kikieo".

The burly big cop shook her making sure there was no blood on his hand. Then over-came the three ATF and Giros. They carried on their back patting for five minutes, then split. Carl had one question and one question only. "When will you get the rest of the Bikers.?"

Romeo grimaced at the question, "They will die soon very, very soon."

CHAPTER 13

Sam and John were loading and unloading weapons and drugs into their new mansion. When Li arrived at their gate with the news of the fallen Foot soldiers and Hand commanders. He was told to go straight to the Bikers and make them aware that Romeo and his friends had won. John crossed over to the gate slipping into shadow just as easy as any Ninja. He appeared shadowy and huge his frame towering over The young Oriental who stood there petrified knowing that all the rumours were true. They ate the dead and fed them to their dogs. They were just as tricky as any Martial artist, They-were armed to the teeth, And the police were not even an even match for them.

So he crossed his fingers and gulped then said, "The Lin Qua are finished in this city,"

John took a gulp of an ice-cold beer and said, "Who is Romeo? Anyway. What clan is he from I don't mean the Tokagure. I mean who has taken on him and the other two into their clan?"

The oriental felt his hair rise on his skin. He was getting a cold sweat down his back. He gulped again and said, "Koga. The clan now work with the aim of getting a new master and that master will be Romeo."

He told this to the giant leather clad biker.

"You'll live," said John and the young Oriental drove off sweating buckets and having a panic attack.

*

Romeo opened the door to his abode and smiled, smelling the sandalwood incense that had been lit to help focus their Ki and make them more in tune, not just with the environment but the Universe as well. They were focusing on their chakras and meridians. Which is all the healing they were allowed. I mean Romeo was a fair hand at acupuncture and massage techniques. But they needed to be quiet and keep their spirits focused. Their energies aligned and one with both spirit and material worlds. They knelt again and began the complex finger knitting exercises this time to warm their spirits down. They needed to rest.

They slept for two days straight. The three of them out for count. Nothing surer than all-out war could wake them. They were silent in their slumber not snoring or breathing heavily. The house was a tomb. Not even the dead could wake them. Romeo once again began to dream. Of ancient days and ancient battles his Lady Julie needing rescued. He was dressed in black with his small armament of Katana and Kama. He began to track the Double headed dragon. Following the burnt-out ruins of various villages leading to the mountain just north of a village that was still in embers. Still burning away. The villagers mostly torched and the rest ripped in half by massive talons and devoured. The smell was acrid and foul. Of a peasant that had been there a while and never hurting or hurt by anyone else. This was how much times were changing. The double headed hydra had grabbed his love out of a monastery she was visiting to pray to the gods for how blessed she was. The monks and clergy had tried to hide her virgin white soul. In bowers of the monastery where they kept their books and other artefacts.

The dream carried on and then faded into oblivion. With him gasping for air after, the arduous task of killing the dragon. Romeo had cut off one head then with power of what must have been godlike, he cleft the dragons heart in two. He woke panting and sore, Kikieo was above him mopping up the sweat that was lashing down his face.

"You woke me," she said.

Romeo rested his head again on her bosom whilst she mopped the sweat of his brow.

"What happened in the dream?" she asked moving his hair from out of his good eye.

"I was hunting a dragon," He said, "It had taken my Julie and was using her for entertainment." Kikieo smiled, "you kill the dragon?"

He smiled at this and replied, "Yes, yes I did."

She let a small wry smile come across her face. "Then you are truly blessed," she continued, "The gods only send visions when the time is right." He blinked a little, she continued "And the fact that you won the battle is a heap of blessings in itself. The gods must be pleased."

He smiled and fell back asleep. His mind and body appeased and spirit intact. Giros was through in the living room sleeping on a bamboo mat. He opened his eyes blinked and listened to the two lovers as they gently spoke to each other, then after they settled down he closed his eyes and fell back asleep.

*

Brian MacArthur was again starting to haunt the three ninja. He knew their next move and the task was arduous and very challenging. He hugged the shadows along the side of Romeos block of flats. Merging deftly and skilfully with the environment. He crouched down and started to use his hands in his traditional Kanji. The ancient form that only he could use. As his master whom he had killed shortly after teaching him the magical kanji. He did this as he was jealous and the secrets could only be passed down by him. And he wasn't in a hurry to do that. He finished the last Kanji making the mystical symbol in the air then drawing to a zen.

*

Romeo bathed then dressed back in black. He began to don his chainmail gauntlets. And pushed through his golden sash, his Kama. Giros smiled and carried on with his wrist and ankle wraps. Kikieo was strapping her Katana to her back. She had spent the best part of an hour envenoming the last of her Shuken. Seven in total, she then donned her hood touched her toes (this was to limber her body up) and then she put on her hood. They then waited for Li the young messenger boy to show up. He would have the address of John and Sam, and the rest of the gang of bikers. The little dirt bike approached. And Li climbed the stairs, again he rapped gently on the door. Romeo opened it and the young man stepped into the shadows.

"Li," came Romeo's voice.

"Yes," was the reply. "The address please."

The young man ripped a parchment of paper and scrawled the address on it. Romeo handed him another thousand dollars, this was danger pay.

*

John and Sam were putting their drug money profits through a money counter fives, first then in ascension up to fifty-dollar bills. Tonnes of cash, enough to keep a small country. Meanwhile in the other room they were cutting the cocaine, speed and heroin. The room a short trip down the hall was their Armoury. They had rocket launchers, sub-machine guns, AK47's the small combat models. Also Glock specials. They even had a couple of chainsaws. Which they would use to full effect on their close combat with numbers. Two out of their minds outlaws chopping into a large crowd of bystanders. It had been used in great effect whilst escaping the law during a particularly dodgy bank raid. It was a devastating tactic that soon showed both police and citizen, that they meant business. Blood ran when these bikers appeared. Most of the gang were ex-army. Special forces.

John walked away from the counting room. And loaded up a combat, four shot pump action shotgun. It was one of his favourites. He also sheathed a wicked jungle machete that was serrated on the other side. He then picked up a couple of fragment grenades. The green ones that sent shrapnel everywhere. Apples he liked to call them. He also loaded up a desert eagle special that was totally chrome and could withstand water. He then produced some PCP and sprinkled a little amount on the muscle that sat between his fore finger and thumb. He snorted it and smiled a wicked evil grin.

Sam was next, Sam was old fashioned when it came to the nitty gritty, He liked his colts, especially the long slide automatic. It only held seven bullets but they were large forty fives and they were hollow points, which meant they shredded on contact. In a splaying pattern. That ripped through the flesh and destroying organs and bones.

"Messy," he said and put three mags into a mag holder around his waist. He then produced a wicked bowie knife which could easily take the head off a young buck deer. They were prepared for the onslaught. Also the love room that they have was being set up with sand bags and a small mini gun. The ones that are usually mounted on the sides of Apache helicopters. That weapon could easily shred through the walls that were concrete blocks. It was showdown time. And John and Sam were determined not to let anything stop them from controlling the city.

Romeo was just a small itch or so they thought. Then it started two whining dogs then silence as they killed the last two rotties. Poison thought John. Sam was not the least bit surprised.

"This Romeo?" Sam said, "Who is he?"

John took another charge of PCP. "Is it who I think it is?"

Sam's eyes went straight and cold, "It's the fucker we raped more than four years ago."

John laughed and said, "Oh you catch on fast".

The thought of him being alive added an extra bit of excitement to the whole scenario. Sam grimaced just as the lights went in the mansion. "Oh we are truly fucked."

He slapped a magazine into the combat AK47. Then cocked it, he wasn't going out like that, he heard the gurgling of one of his brothers as he died. The blood spilling out of his mouth as his lung was ruptured.

*

Romeo stared into the soul of the large biker, watching the light go out in his eyes. Kikieo on the other hand had produced a razor sharp Tanto and slipped the weapon across one of the biker's throat, from behind. This sent a slick of blood down the man's jacket and onto the floor. She let go of the man and he slumped next to the puddle of blood, dead. Giros on the other hand was heading across to the armoury. Silently and on half feet and cat feet. Shortening his stride and listening very carefully. He tuned in on breathing patterns. Listening, trying to see how many were in the room. He closed his eyes and focused. 'Three' he thought. And slid his back along the wall next to the door frame. He stood waiting for one of them to come through the doorway. He was right three of them the first walked out the door. Giros pulled the man, and at the same instant pushed a Sai through the man's heart. Killing him instantly. He then with a stealthy movement moved the corpse of the biker next to him, so as not to alert the other two.

They came next and again Giros struck, simultaneously digging the razor-sharp blades of the Sai into each of their abdomens. Right through their Hara. Each of the men groaned and Giros pulled the blades out of them. Then the next second a lump of the wall exploded next to Giro's. He was being shot at by Sam. The large calibre pistol, sliding and expelling the shells as the weapon cracked off bullet after bullet. But Giros tucked into a forward roll. And dodged the bullets,

Sam grimaced as he loaded another magazine. And repeatedly shot the weapon at Giros who rolled right onto the porch, noticing Romeo beside the doorway. Romeo ducked into a low stance and threw one of his Shurikens at Sam. It caught the big bear like frame of Sam just under his clavicle. Romeo vanished into the shadows. As did Giros. They were going to re-group. Kikieo came next back flipping gently in and out the shadows. Making very little to no sound at all.

John seeing the hit that Sam took, and knowing that those Shuriken were usually laced with poison poured whisky on the wound to clean it.

"So much for a stand-up fight," John said as he began to stitch up the wound. "You'll live," he continued. "Half my brothers are dead, and you might be poisoned."

"We got to turn this fight around."

"Yeah well the good thing is we don't have to worry about the triads."

John finished stitching Sam, "yeah but that means more leg work for us. And some of the customers that were the triads. Well they will be getting brave," Sam grimaced as he put his shirt back on, then the leather waistcoat.

"We should hit that fucking Romeo tonight," said Sam, John gave a little shrug as to say 'Whatever'.

*

Romeo put the miniature alarm at the foot of the stairs. So he could hear the coming and goings, of not just the neighbours but also anyone else. He was wondering whether Carl and the ATF would be stopping to see him soon. Romeo had a feeling that they would be round soon to dot the i's and cross the t's. Romeo laid his Kama to rest and smiled as he rung the Chinese take away for a feast.

Romeo sat down in half lotus as did Giro's and Kikieo. The ate the cuisine, which was a banquet as news of the victory over the Lin Qua was fast and truthful. They only had John and Sam to worry about. But these things were in hand.

Romeo started to cough a little. The food wasn't poisoned it was just the HIV was beginning to take hold. Then he looked at his thigh. There was a small scratch that was tingling. He now knew that Brian was as deceitful as any snake. He had done the damage and the toxin was pneumonia. He could tell he was in trouble. He began to feel the fever growing. This wasn't like heroin addiction, no this was a finisher and he knew it. He went straight to the phone and dialled his brother-in-law who had just come out the army. He was a recon delta with a Bramley's, conditioning which meant he was tough and ruff enough to handle any situation. He kept his beret for his safety. He only told Romeo certain things. But Romeo knew that was only for his safety.

Romeo smiled as he spoke Japanese to his brother-in-law. Jason spoke back to him quietly being careful as not to offend him as the conversation was a deep one.

"Yes Jason it's pneumonia. I haven't got long left. It's a superbug."

Jason grimaced and said shit to himself as the cough racked Romeo's body. He then said to Romeo. "I take it you want to finish of the spirit training."

Romeo pulled himself together and laughed, "I think so don't you Jason".

Jason laughed back, "I'll be there in two days. The brass know your predicament and I will be granted compassionate leave."

Romeo gave a small, satisfied sigh, "you better hurry".

Jason smiled and hung up. He went straight operational supervisor. They had already signed his leave on the grounds of family bereavement. He walked in the office and before he even spoke, the Chief handed him his state of grace, they knew everything. He about turned and went and got his civilian clothes and left the naval yard. And drove to the airport. His plane was in forty minutes. He boarded the plane which would get him to the city of Los Angeles, where he would pick up his specialist equipment and at the same time he would pay homage to his sister and nephew by laying flowers on the grave. He was a lithe wiry man with a Gung Ho. Look as if to say, 'Don't fucking mess.' If he shot you a thousand-yard stare it meant, 'Don't mess cause I'm blessed dressed and know the best' and if you do anything to insult me I'll show you hell in three ticks.

He gathered his martial arts weapons and various suits for three different schools. Muay Thai, Chinese shadow boxing and Japanese ninjitsu. He was an expert in the lore of each school. But the spiritual side was a fair bit away from completion. Now he had to summon the Shinobi spirit of the dragon this meant kneeling meditation in a room with very little light. He sat as the Chinese sandalwood burnt into the rooms atmosphere.

He began spirit shaping and low growls of words and ancient hand movements. Speciality training. In the highest respect of the three schools of Martial science. He was known for three things. One was sniper training the other was disappearing without a trace. The last was multiple attacks without having to breathe. He always blacked out at the end of said skill. They call it master of dragons. It was a series of Muay Thai, tai chi, ninja yoga and subtle shadow deception of Chinese Wu Shu. He only had another seven ways to interconnect the styles and become true Shinobi. Romeo was guiding him to be a true Shinobi. Every time Jason Kendricks got shore leave he studied with Romeo. But Romeo had kept it secret, and never told anyone about what went on in private with Jason. It was hours of study. That of honing his senses never relying on all of his instincts. But knowing which ones were optimum, and what where not in use. It takes great strength to hone the five senses and give you a sixth sense a shadowy world where very few knew what to do to survive. In this world It was the transference of Ninja to Shinobi and Shinobi to ancient spiritual warrior of Jian.

Such skills have only been heard of no one has ever seen this warrior state of both history and evolution. Not many knew this shadowy world and most were put off by the fear of such dedication of this Martial Art. Jian were old monks that took there fierce training and became the most skilled assassins in the world. Jason carried on his meditation. A full day and night kneeling. Focusing on that shadowy world and staying relaxed. It took years of dedication. And months of preparation. That's why he was so exonerated in the USA marine corp. His skill was unmatched. It took the colonels and other ranks a lot of energy to keep up with him, He was a shadow a wraith. A mystical warrior. A Shinobi of the highest level. No you didn't ask anything of the Ninja because he might just deliver. So much so they kept tabs on him as much as they could. But this was family. And personal. Meditation came to an end and all that was left was his travelling to Romeo.

Romeo fever grew more as the night followed day. He was lashing sweat and every now and then a cough racked his body and caused him to convulsive. He lay still after about four hours of mucus and laboured breathing, and coughing fits. Kikieo was mopping his forehead and feeling the various pulse points. Specifically his lungs, she fed him ancient remedies brewed by The Chinese doctor. Mainly herbs. She also massaged his back as she held him close.

She whispered, "I love you". in Japanese.

He responded in kind with a rough cracked voice. "Thank you," he replied.

She lay him back down on his futon. Giros looked on with a solemn gaze. "Romeo San," he said, "Is your brother-in-law as good as you say?"

Romeo laughed and said, "Better".

Giros nodded his head in an affirmative way, "Good Romeo San very good. You had it covered, knowing that you had been outdone, the moment that Brian MacArthur had entered the battle."

Romeo stood up knowing he had to prepare for Jason. He walked over to where his Gi and weapons lay. He reached in and got the shuriken and the chain mail gauntlets. He seized over and began to cough. Giros rushed to catch him but Romeo put out his hand as to say 'I'm okay' with his other hand he wiped a smear of blood that had come up from his lungs. He began to unwrap the two Kama that were his favourite weapons. He looked to see if his soul still shone on the crescent moon blades. He was looking for the blue tinge that shone on the steel. If he was correct and hoping like hell that he was he would last a fortnight and be able to complete Jason's training. And hopefully the four of them would finish Sam and John. Then he could go back to rest in peace and join his angelic wife.

He knelt and summoned his Ki, he began to interlock his fingers making first the sign chi, then the dragon and after that he folded fire and heated up his Ki. Stoking it with wood then turning the Dao clockwise. Then dismissing it with a clap. Then again the Ki and lighting it with the dragon. Stoking it with wood then adding a little of metal. Then he clapped after turning the Dao clockwise. And started the ritual this time adding more metal. He could feel his meridians pumping and beating. Putting both a stop to the cough and the lungs from drowning. He calmly pulled himself into a zen state of pure consciousness. He sat that way until the smoky figure came to his house. This was the next day. The door opened and Jason walked in keeping to his shadows side. And immersing himself in said shadows.

Romeo smiled and said quietly, "Jason San".

Jason smiled under his hood, "Okay Romeo, How long until you perish."

He said then knelt next to the dragon covered body, of Romeo.

"I have managed to hold the disease off for a few days, five tops. I have managed to quell the superbug and using all my Ki energies. I have stopped it doubling over and drowning my lungs with mucus."

Jason could see the drenching of his body in sweat.

"I take it you didn't count on Brian being so stealthy. And having a bio tech weapon."

Romeo stood up and showed his thigh off. Then pointed to a small cut at the back of his elbow, "No didn't count on him having two."

Jason grimaced at the thought of all the training that Romeo had immersed himself in. The power and the will of his soul. That will be released on his death. And the martial arts world would go into mourning. Romeo would become a legend a historical part of the martial arts world.

*

John and Sam and about twelve of his chapter turned the road towards Romeo's apartment. The noise of their iron horses was deafening. It was about half two in the afternoon. And very, very warm. They all got off their bikes. And John smiled in an evil grin. "Lock and load boys."

Sam got off his chopper and started to pull the chord of a chainsaw. He looked up the stairwell as the chainsaw began to rev up and sputter. Then kicked into life.

"Wheee wheee wheee piggy's" He then began to ascend the stairs.

The rest of the chapter all laughed as they heard him get louder and louder the closer he got to the top. Then he pushed the saw through the door sending up sawdust. And sending the door to pieces. As he pushed the saw through the door it fell apart. Romeo was quick and sent two of his deadly Shuken straight at Sam, who managed to dodge one but the other went straight into the man's chest just below the giant biker's clavicle. Jason was next, he flung some blinding powder right into the bikers eyes. He dropped the saw and Kikieo was next to strike sending a blade straight through his heart. Giros was last and severed the head off the monster's shoulders.

"No more, big bad wolf," said Romeo and as he switched off the chainsaw an evil silence befell the area. Jason produced three or four Shuriken smiled under his hood, pointed down stairs and said quietly. "We take the rest now?"

Romeo thought about it and replied, "Yeah either that or retreat to safety".

Jason produced his Katana and said, "I'm up for either".

Romeo began to cough a little. A small smudge of blood was left on his palm. He stopped coughing and whispered. "Time is never time enough".

They then descended to the bottom of the stairwell. And the four of them slipped silently into the shadows, Giros an Kikieo sidled to the left while Romeo and Jason slid to the right. They didn't make a sound. They decided to use a pincer manoeuvre. So they were safe in the shadows. They began to make their stand. Romeo smiled as the bikers had suddenly gone quiet. Not even a bird song, as the air hung heavy with the sweat and leather of the bikers. But they had just realised that these were spiritual assassins they were facing. And something cold and sinister was crawling down each of their backs.

John began to walk towards the stairwell. The ninjas hid in the shadows and let the monstrous figure of John carry on past and up the stairs. "Sam?" he shouted as he walked up the stairs. "Sam where are you brother?" He got to the doorway and saw his compadre's body with its head lying next to the corpse. John gave a loud shrill whistle and shouted on his brotherhood to come up.

Romeo and the other three smiled at the classic blunder they had just made. They had boxed themselves into the stairwell. The four ninja began the craft of carnage, taking the chapter in surprise. The four ninja hacked and severed limbs, and cut through torsos. It was like shooting fish in a barrel. The bikers didn't even get the chance to realise they had made such a foolish blunder. The stairwell was turned into a river of blood. They eventually got to John who was cowering in fear. He had been in fights but didn't realise that Romeo was as skilled as he was. Romeo didn't hesitate, he gripped his Kama and swung it through the bikers neck decapitating him, a jet of blood gushed up as the main veins in the head and neck were severed. Romeo smiled under his hood and thought Julie will be waiting.

Romeo rested in peace and let the life ebb out of his body.

THE END

www.ingramcontent.com/pod-product-compliance
Lightning Source LLC
Chambersburg PA
CBHW020149180626
46810CB00004B/1808